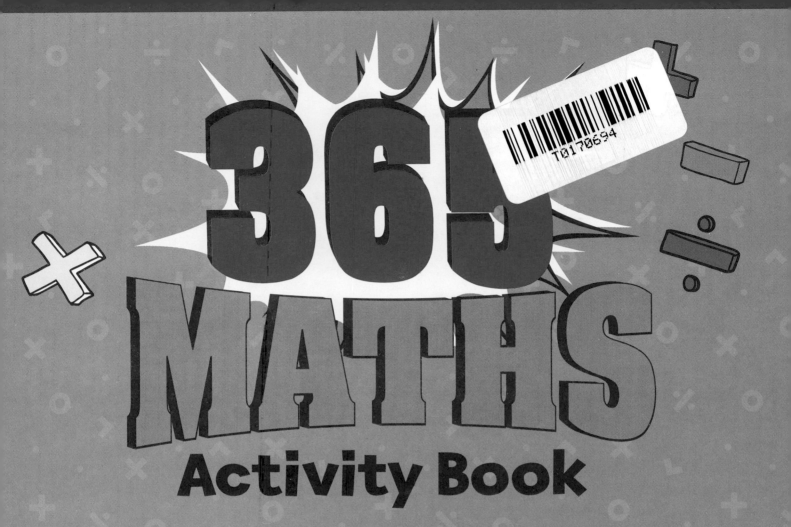

365 MATHS
Activity Book

This book belongs to

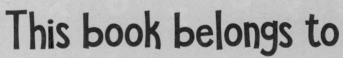

Wonder House

Wonder House

(An imprint of Prakash Books)

contact@wonderhousebooks.com

ISBN : 978-93-54403-03-3

Introduction

Children often find mathematics difficult. The concepts are too confusing, they say. `I do not understand it, it's too hard,' is something often heard. But there is nothing more fun, practical and engaging than mathematics once you understand the concepts and their application.

A child's first introduction to math is through numbers. As they move forward, in school, these numbers become bigger. It is not so long before children are introduced to, are learning and applying advanced concepts like subtraction, multiplication and the like in class and in real world. Some among them perhaps are still at odds with the subject.

365 *Maths Activity Book* plays a dual role to make mathematics fun for children. The book not only introduces children to various concepts but it also gives them ample amount of exercises to practice their understanding of the concepts. The various concepts are explained keeping their difficulty level in mind, which is gradually increased. Further, the interrelation between the various concepts is also explained in the book. Concepts in this book range from addition, subtraction, introduction to multiplication, comparing, fractions and even tables. Concepts of time, money and measurement are also explained in an easy manner and has ample practice.

Understanding Concepts

Addition

Addition is to find out how much or quantity of an object.
It is like counting things to know their quantity and reach a number.
The sign or symbol of addition is +.

This is how we do addition:

$3 + 2 = 5$

+ = **5**

Subtraction

Subtraction is to find out the difference between two numbers.
It is to compare the quantities of two objects.
The sign or symbol of subtraction is −.

This is how we do subtraction:

$3 - 2 = 1$

− = **1**

Multiplication

To multiply is to add together groups of the same number.
It is faster to add numbers in groups rather than counting them one at a time.
The sign or symbol of multiplication is **x**.

This is how we do multiplication:

$3 \times 3 = 9$

x 3 = 9

is same as

+ + = 9

Division

Division is splitting an object into equal parts or groups.
It is also combining and dividing two numbers to make a new number.
Sometimes when we divide, a number still remains that cannot be divided into equal parts.
The sign or symbol of division is ÷.

This is how we do division:

$6 \div 2 = 3$

÷ 2 = 3

Number line

Number line is used to count, add and subtract.
You can add by counting up the number line and subtract by counting back.

$4 + 3 = 7$

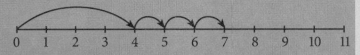

For Addition go this way ⟶

$7 - 4 = 3$

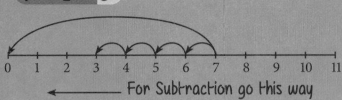

⟵ For Subtraction go this way

Ordinal numbers

These numbers tell us about the position of an object.
They go as, **first, second, third** and so on.

Cardinal numbers

These numbers tell us about the quantity or count of objects.
Numbers written in digits are cardinal numbers.
They go as, **1, 2, 3, 4** and so on.

Place value

Each digit in a number has a place.
The number line describes the position or place of a digit in a number.
The order of place value of digits in a number is read from right to left.

It goes as,

T	H	T	O	Thousand	Hundred	Tens	Ones
2	3	4	7	2	3	4	7

Here, **7** is at the **ONES** position, **4** is at the **TENS** position, **3** is at the **HUNDREDS** position and **2** is at the **THOUSANDS** position.

Fraction

Fraction is a part of something.
You make fraction by splitting something into equal parts.

The bottom number tells us about how many equal parts a thing has been divided into.

The top number tells us about how many parts we have.

| 1 | $\frac{1}{2}$ | $\frac{1}{3}$ | $\frac{1}{4}$ |

| one full | one half | one third | one fouth or quarter |

Number Game

1. Fill in the numbers that come before and after the given numbers.

a.

24

b.

56

2. Count the number of petals on each flower and write the number on the pot.

a.   b.   c.

4. 5 Seeds were planted in each pot. How many still need to grow? Draw and write the number below.

a.

b.

3. Draw each bee's route to the purple flower, following the instructions.

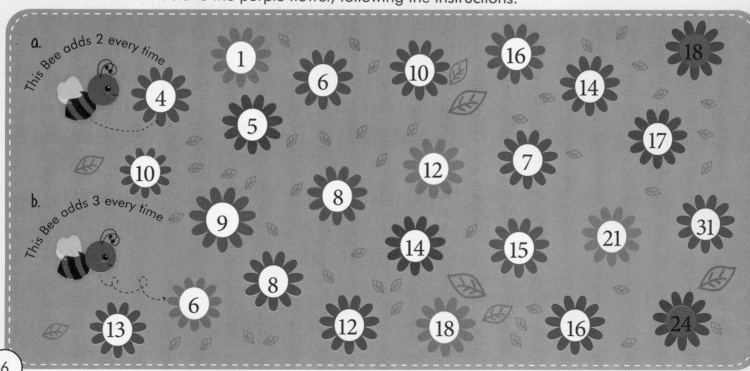

a. This Bee adds 2 every time

4   1   6   10   16   18

5   14

10   12   7   17

b. This Bee adds 3 every time

9   8

14   15   21   31

6

13   8   12   18   16   24

5. Count and circle the correct number.

a.

5	3	7

b.

1	5	6

c.

5	3	2

d.

5	6	7

e.
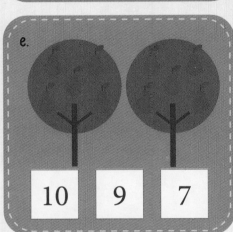

10	9	7

f.
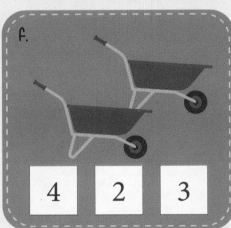

4	2	3

6. Count carefully and answer the questions given below.

a. How many more black ants are there than red ants?

b. How many more butterflies are there than bees?

c. How many more ladybirds are there than grasshoppers?

7. Fill in the missing numbers.

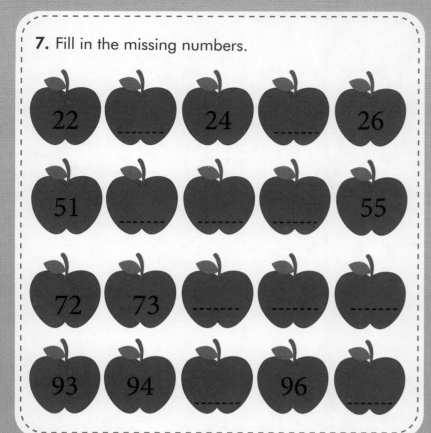

22	_____	24	_____	26
51	_____	_____	_____	55
72	73	_____	_____	_____
93	94	_____	96	_____

9. Skip count by 5 and 10 and write the numbers that come after.

a.

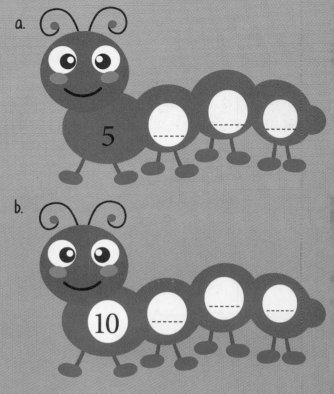

5 _____ _____ _____

b.

10 _____ _____ _____

8. Color by numbers.

① ② ③ ④ ⑤ ⑥ ⑦ ⑧

10. Count and color the fruits. Write their number in the space given below.

○ ○ ○ ○ ○

11. Word Problems.

a. There are 6 bees putting nectar in a bee hive.
3 more bees joined them.
How many bees are there now?

There are ◯

bees putting nectar now.

b. There were 5 birds sitting on a branch.
2 birds flew away.
How many birds are there now?

There are ◯

birds on the branch.

c. There were 5 pears on the tree.
1 pear dropped from the pear tree.
How many pears are there on the tree now?

There are ◯

pears on the tree now.

d. There were 10 eggs in the crate.
The man dropped 2 eggs by mistake.
How many eggs are there in the crate now?

There are ◯

eggs in the crate now.

12. Number word practise.

| One | Three | Ten | Fourteen | Nine |
| Seven | Eleven | Two | Twenty | Six |

 1   3   7   10   11

14 2 20 9 6

13. Match the number names.

 1 ○   ○ Twenty

 7 ○   ○ Six

 6 ○   ○ Five

 20 ○   ○ Seven

 18 ○   ○ Fourteen

 5 ○   ○ One

 14 ○   ○ Eighteen

Number Order

14. Count and write the number of leaves in the pots given below. Color the leaves of the pot that has the greater number of leaves.

a.

b.

16. Compare each set of numbers. use <, >.

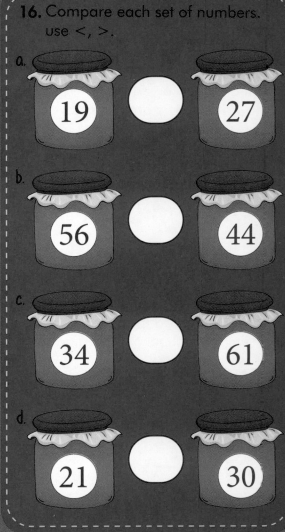

a. 19 ◯ 27

b. 56 ◯ 44

c. 34 ◯ 61

d. 21 ◯ 30

15. Write the numbers in ascending order.

42   74   3   67

Number order

Ascending order.
• Arranging numbers from smallest to largest.

Descending order.
• Arranging numbers from largest to smallest.

10

17. Arrange the numbers written on the pumpkin cart in ascending and descending order on the pumpkin line.

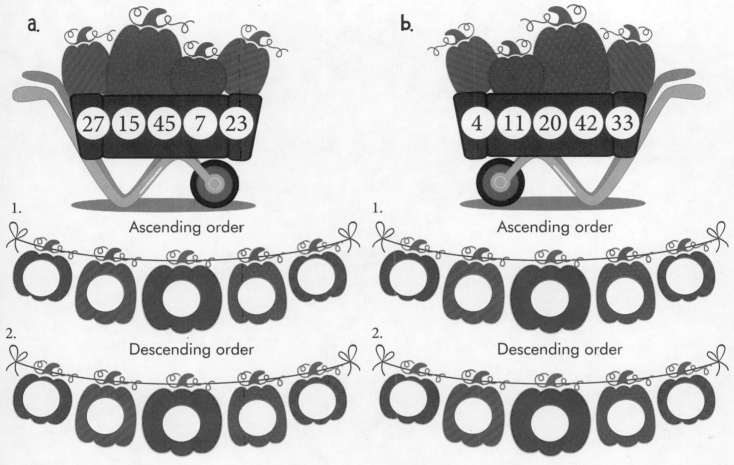

a.

27 15 45 7 23

1. Ascending order

2. Descending order

b.

4 11 20 42 33

1. Ascending order

2. Descending order

18. Ordinal number names.

Color the **First** corn yellow.

Color the **Second** corn orange.

Color the **Third** corn red.

Color the **Fourth** corn pink.

Color the **Fifth** corn purple.

Color the **Sixth** corn green.

Color the **Seventh** corn brown.

Color the **Eighth** corn light blue.

Color the **Ninth** corn light green.

Color the **Tenth** corn gray.

1. 2. 3. 4. 5.

6. 7. 8. 9. 10.

19. Follow the instructions given in the bubbles and see where the animals land. Then fill the answers in the spaces given below.

a. $2 + 8 =$ ◯

b. $13 - 4 =$ ◯

c. $16 - 5 =$ ◯

d. $20 - 5 =$ ◯

e. $11 + 2 =$ ◯

f. $10 + 6 =$ ◯

20. Match the numbers in line A with the numbers in line B that comes after them.

A. a. 45 b. 15 c. 50 d. 25 e. 22 f. 12

B. 16 51 46 23 13 26

21. In the picture code each sea animal stands for a number. Find and write their number in the space given next to their picture.

a.  + + = 3 | = ( )

b. + + = 4 | = ( )

c. + + = 6 | = ( )

d. + + = 9 | = ( )

22. Draw a trail from the sums on the flowers that have the same sum as the number on the bee.

13   12   5   9 d.

a.   b. 6+7   c.   3+2

9+3   4+5

Number Line

★ It is a straight line with numbers placed at equal intervals. It helps in addition and subtraction by counting forwards for addition and backwards for subtraction.

Revise the Example

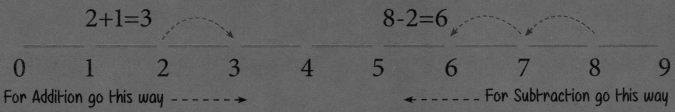

$$2+1=3 \qquad 8-2=6$$

0   1   2   3   4   5   6   7   8   9

For Addition go this way - - - - - - →   ← - - - - - - For Subtraction go this way

23. Draw the jumps on the number line, then color the Easter egg where the bunny finishes and write the answer in the box.

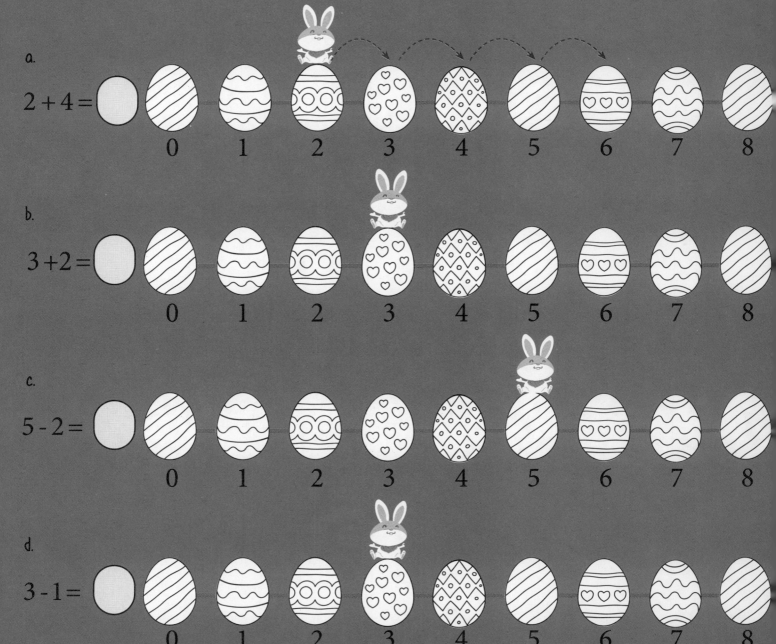

a.

$2 + 4 =$ ⬭

0   1   2   3   4   5   6   7   8

b.

$3 + 2 =$ ⬭

0   1   2   3   4   5   6   7   8

c.

$5 - 2 =$ ⬭

0   1   2   3   4   5   6   7   8

d.

$3 - 1 =$ ⬭

0   1   2   3   4   5   6   7   8

24. Add the cost of each object in the jar and write the answer in the box given below.

use label for rough work

a.

b.

c.

 = 5

= 2

= 3

= 6

- - - - - - - -
Total

- - - - - - - -
Total

- - - - - - - -
Total

25. Color the cupcake that has the greater number in each set.

a.
 2   9

b.
4   11

26. Fill in the missing numbers on the ice cream scoopes with the help of the number line. The numbers at the bottom add up to the number on top.

a.
 7
2 + 5

b.
 8 4

c.
 9
7

d.
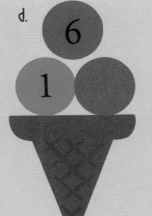 6
1

e.
 2 3

15

27. Solve and write.

a. 2 →+2→ →+4→ →+6→ →+8→ →+10→

b. 3 →+1→ →+3→ →+5→ →+7→ →+9→

c. 4 →+1→ →+4→ →+3→ →+2→ →+5→

d. 5 →+2→ →+5→ →+1→ →+4→ →+3→

28. Solve and write the missing numbers.

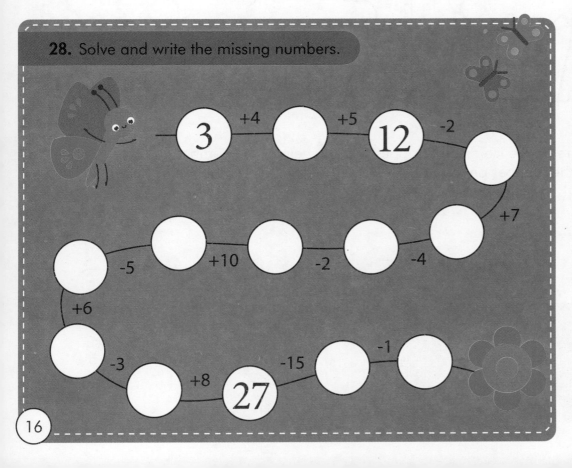

3 →+4→ ◯ →+5→ 12 →-2→ ◯ →+7→ ◯ →-4→ ◯ →-2→ ◯ →+10→ ◯ →-5→ ◯ →+6→ ◯ →-3→ ◯ →+8→ 27 →-15→ ◯ →-1→ ◯

29. If it is true then color 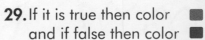 and if false then color ■

a. | 3 | = | 3 | ☐

b. | 5 | < | 4 | ☐

c. | 6 | < | 8 | ☐

d. | 1 | > | 4 | ☐

e. | 9 | = | 7 | ☐

30. Solve and write.

 = 3   = 2    = 4   = 6

 − = ☐

 − = ☐

☐ − ☐ = ☐

☐ − ☐ = ☐

31. Add the numbers and write the answer in the given space.

a.

b.

32. Match with the correct answer.

a. 5+2   b. 7−4   c. 8−2   d. 6+5

 11

 6

7

3

a.   b.   c.   d.

Knowing Numbers

33. Color the candies with odd answers as red and with even answers as blue.

a. 13+5= ◯

b. 6+8= ◯

c. 7+4= ◯

d. 11+5= ◯

e. 26-9= ◯

f. 21-9= ◯

g. 27-7= ◯

h. 30+9= ◯

34. Count and write the sum of the odd and even heart candies that you see inside the jar.

Odd ◯   Even ◯

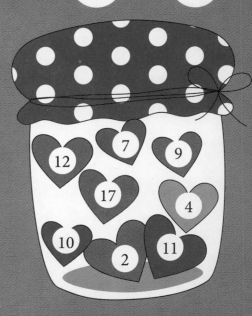

12   7   9   17   4   10   2   11

35. Write the expanded form of the numbers along with their number names and place values.

a.

986 I am expanding.

My number name is

_____

I have

.....hundreds..... tens .....ones

_____

My expanded form is

_____ + _____ + _____

b.

116 I am expanding.

My number name is

_____

I have

.....hundreds..... tens .....ones

_____

My expanded form is

_____ + _____ + _____

c.

208 I am expanding.

My number name is

_____

I have

.....hundreds..... tens .....ones

_____

My expanded form is

_____ + _____ + _____

36. Color the monster with the even number.

a.
13

b.
6

c.
11

d.
7

37. Write the place value of the digit marked with the dotted line.

a.
349 _____

b.
614 _____

c.
490 _____

d.
831 _____

e.
114 _____

f.
254 _____

38. Help the baby monsters solve the place value word problem.

a.

I am an even number

I am between 20-30

My ones digit is 8

What am I?

I am _____ _____

b.

I am between 35-45

I have 3 in tens place

My digit total is 9

What am I?

I am _____ _____

c.

I am not an even number

My ones digit is 1

I have 5 tens

What am I?

I am _____ _____

19

39. Which number comes next?

a.

9   18   27   -----

b.

13   26   39   -----

c.

6   12   18   -----

40. Identify the pattern and write the missing numbers.

a.

4   8   12   -----

b.

7   14   -----   28

c.

5   -----   15   20

d.

-----   20   30   40

41. Add spots on the butterflies equal to the answer of the sum problem given below and color it.

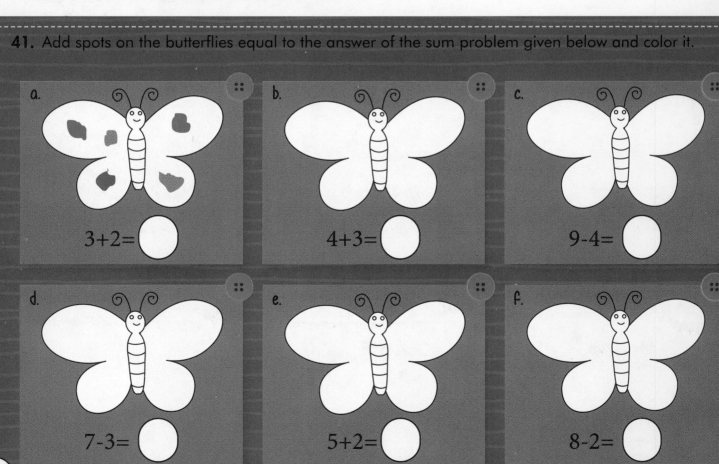

a.   3+2=◯

b.   4+3=◯

c.   9-4=◯

d.   7-3=◯

e.   5+2=◯

f.   8-2=◯

42. Write the numbers that come before and after the given digits and color the cherries brightly.

a.
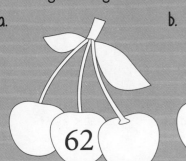
62

b.

91

c.

49

d.

12

e.

83

f.

70

43. Add the numbers on the petals and write the answer in the center.

a.
2 1
3 2
6

b.

7 2
1 5
9

c.
5 3
8 1
4

d.

4 1
2 5
9

44. Match the rat with the pumpkin that has equivalent sum as on the rat.

a.

18

b.

2

c.
25

d.
17

1.
11+7

2.

20-3

3.

8-6

4.
16+9

21

Addition/Subtraction Order

45. Solve addition and subtraction problems.

a.
3+1= ◯

b.
14-3= ◯

c.
5+2= ◯

d.
8-3= ◯

e.
5+4= ◯

f.
12-2= ◯

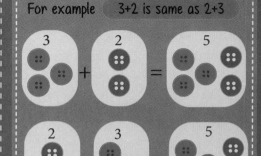

In **Addition** we can put the numbers in any order.

For example   3+2 is same as 2+3

| 3 | 2 | 5 |
| + | = | |

| 2 | 3 | 5 |
| + | = | |

For **Subtraction**, always start with the first number.

For example   3-2 is not same as 2-3

| 3 | 2 | 1 |
| - | = | |

| 2 | 3 | -1 |
| - | = | ✕ |

46. Practise addition and subtraction.

a.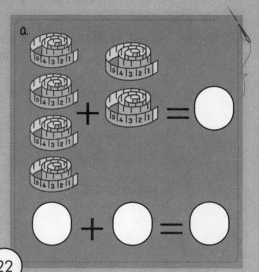

b.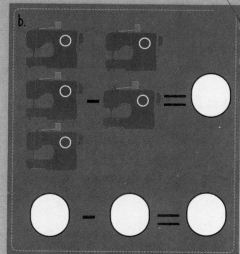

c.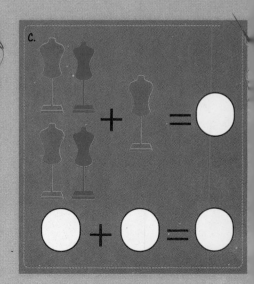

47. Solve the puzzle.

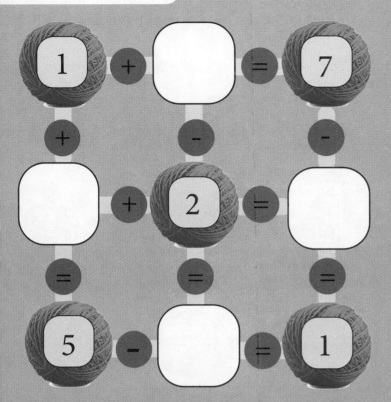

$1 + \square = 7$

$\square + 2 = \square$

$5 - \square = 1$

48. Match the upper and lower half of the eggs and color them with the same color.

a. 8

3+5

2+5

1+4

e. 5

4+2

6+3

c. 6

b. 9

d. 7

49. Solve the problems and color the number of pictures equal to the answer.

a.
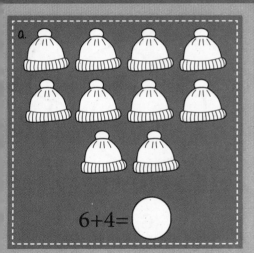
6+4= ◯

b.
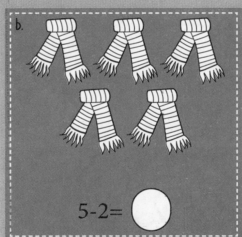
5-2= ◯

c.

5+4= ◯

d.
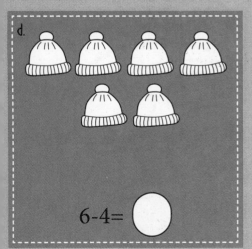
6-4= ◯

e.
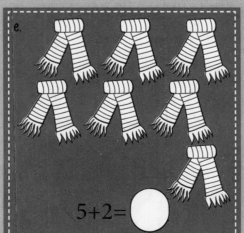
5+2= ◯

f.
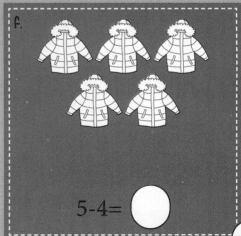
5-4= ◯

23

50. Solve the problems and write the answer in the space given on the top.

a.

9+6

b.

8+5

c.

15-10

d.

16-5

51. Solve the problems and match the fruit that has the same answer as on the baskets given below.

a. 7+8   b. 20-2   c. 5+5   d. 14-4

e. 18-3   f. 10+5   g. 12-2   h. 13+2

10   15   18

52. Solve and color by numbers.

2+1 =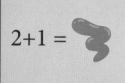

4-2 =

1+3 =

5-4 =

1+4 =

3+3 =

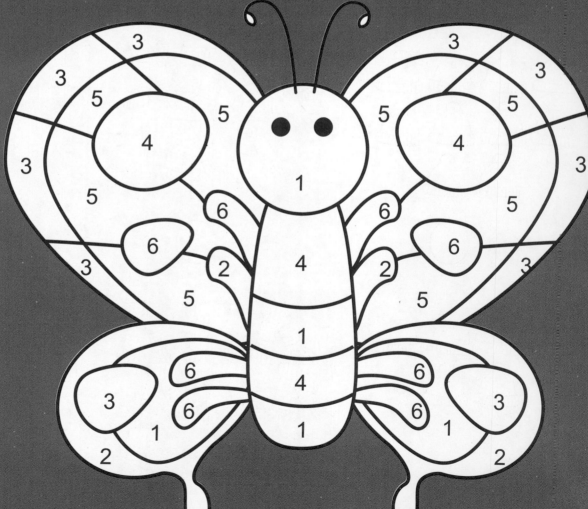

24

53. Solve the picture code puzzle and write the number in the space given.

 $+$ = 10

 $+$ = 15

 $+$ = 14

 $+$ =

54. Check if the equation is true or false.

If true color red 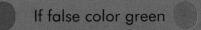 If false color green

a. 5+3=8

b. 7+4=10

c. 5+6=9

d. 7-2=5

e. 12-6=7

f. 10-3=7

55. Figure out the price of the fruits given on each plate. The price of the fruits are given next to their picture. Use the space given below for calculations.

 9 7 3 4 1

10 5 8 6 2

a.

b.

c.

d.

25

56. Write the sum of the two numbers on the robot.

a. 15 +6 ◯

b. 27 -4 ◯

c. 32 +5 ◯

d. 20 -7 ◯

57. Fill in the box with the correct add or subtract sign.

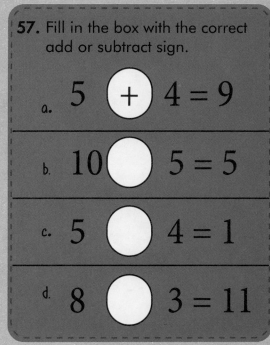

a. 5 (+) 4 = 9

b. 10 ◯ 5 = 5

c. 5 ◯ 4 = 1

d. 8 ◯ 3 = 11

58. Solve the problem from left to right and fill the missing numbers.

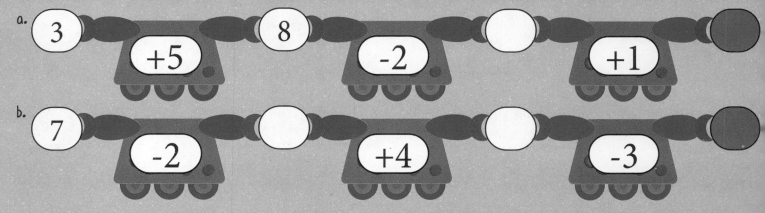

a. 3 +5 8 -2 ◯ +1 ◯

b. 7 -2 ◯ +4 ◯ -3 ◯

59. Add all the numbers on each figure and write the answer in the box given on the figure.

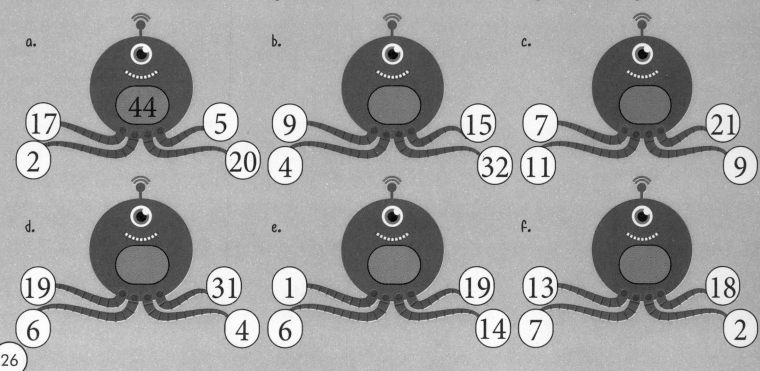

a. 44 — 17, 2, 5, 20

b. 9, 4, 15, 32

c. 7, 11, 21, 9

d. 19, 6, 31, 4

e. 1, 6, 19, 14

f. 13, 7, 18, 2

26

60. Solve the problems and color by number.

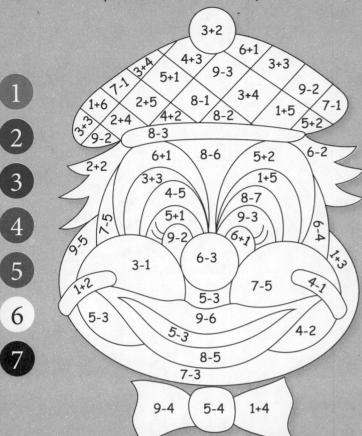

1
2
3
4
5
6
7

61. Balance the scale such that both sides have the same answer for the different sums.

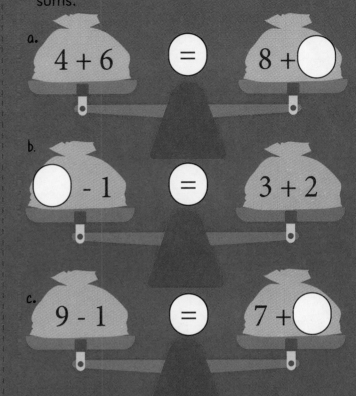

a. $4 + 6$ = $8 + \bigcirc$

b. $\bigcirc - 1$ = $3 + 2$

c. $9 - 1$ = $7 + \bigcirc$

62. Solve the word problems.

a. Hope had 13 apples in a basket. She later put 7 more apples in it. How many apples are in the basket now?

There are $\bigcirc$ apples in the basket.

b. Jack had 10 coins in his pocket. He gets 5 more coins from his mother. How many coins does he have now?

He has $\bigcirc$ coins in his pocket.

c. There are 15 boys and 13 girls in the classroom. How many children are there altogether?

There are $\bigcirc$ children altogether.

d. There were 18 donuts in the box. We ate 10 donuts. How many are left in the box now?

There are $\bigcirc$ donuts left in the box.

63. Add all the numbers given on the ball and write the answer.

a.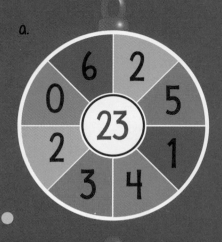

b.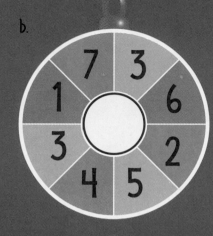

c.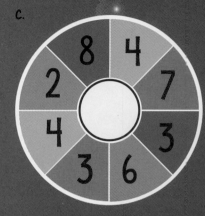

d.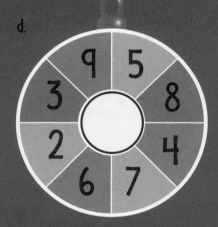

e.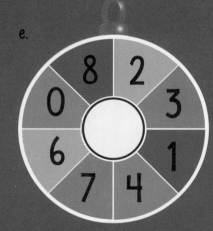

f.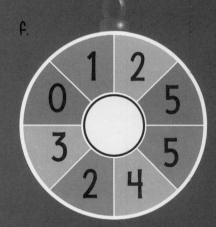

64. Solve and write.

a. 32 + 45 - 12 =

b. 65 + 14 + 6 =

c. 78 - 23 + 43 =

65. Solve the word problems.

a. Lucy bought 15 gifts for Christmas. She gave 6 to her sister Annie. How many gifts are left now?

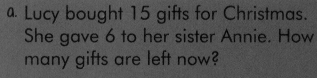

b. Mike started decorating the Christmas tree at 4. It took him 3 hours to decorate it. What is the time now?

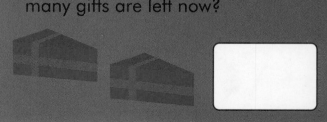

66. Trace the lines, count the lights and write the answer.

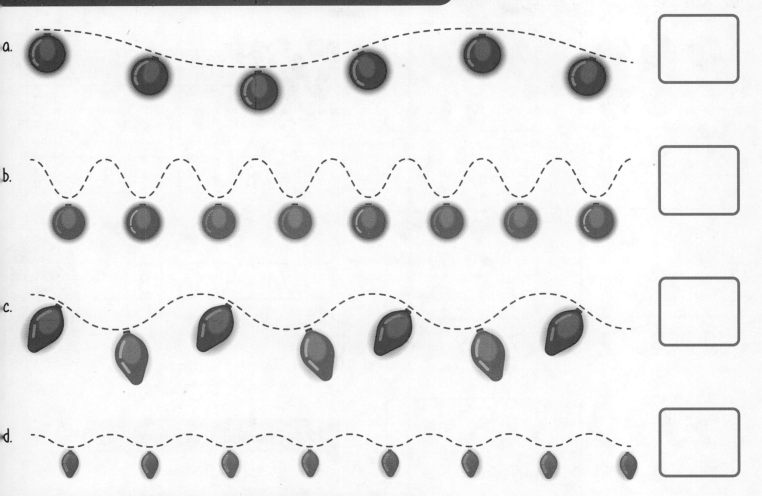

a. ☐

b. ☐

c. ☐

d. ☐

67. Study the pattern and write the missing numbers.

a. 42 ◯ 38 ◯

b. 64 ◯ ◯ 67

c. 78 83 ◯ ◯

68. Color by number.

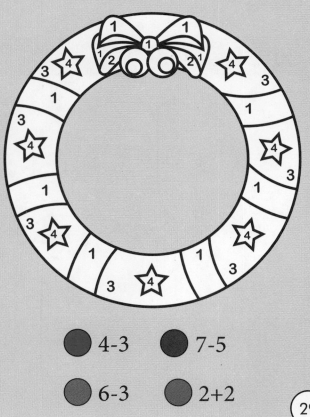

● 4-3   ● 7-5

● 6-3   ● 2+2

29

a.

1 5 3

b.

6 5 7

c.

3 2 1

d.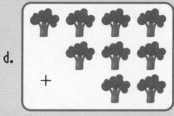

7 9 8

e.

6 5 4

f.

1 5 4

70. Solve and reach the barn.

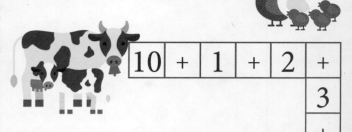

10	+	1	+	2	+
					3
					+

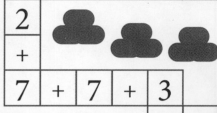

+	8	+	1	+	5	+	4
2							
+							
7	+	7	+	3			
			=				

71. Count and write.

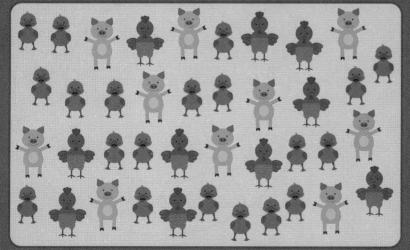

a.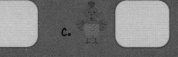

b.

c.

72. Solve and write the answers.

a. 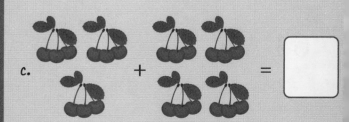 + =

b. + =

c. + =

d. + =

30

73. Fill in the missing numbers on the barn window. Add the numbers at the bottom to get your answer.

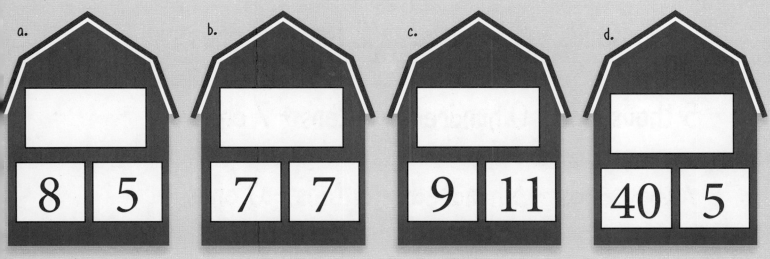

a.

| 8 | 5 |

b.

| 7 | 7 |

c.

| 9 | 11 |

d.

| 40 | 5 |

74. Count and solve.

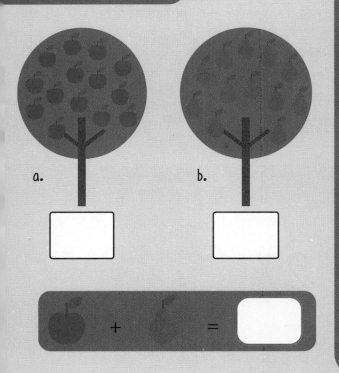

a.

b.

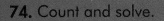

+ =

75. Fill in the missing numbers by adding 2 to the previous number.

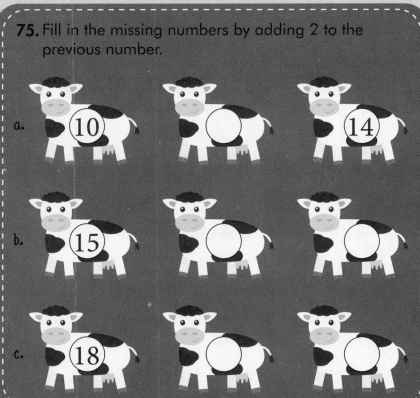

a. 10 ___ 14

b. 15 ___ ___

c. 18 ___ ___

76. Color the ones whose sum adds up to 8.

a. 1+6   b. 5+3   c. 2+7   d. 4+4

31

77. Write the numbers using the place values.

a. 6 thousands + 5 hundreds + 2 tens + 4 ones =

b. 5 thousands + 0 hundreds + 1 tens + 7 ones =

c. 7 thousands + 3 hundreds + 4 tens + 0 ones =

d. 8 thousands + 4 hundreds + 3 tens + 1 ones =

e. 4 thousands + 6 hundreds + 8 tens + 3 ones =

f. 2 thousands + 5 hundreds + 6 tens + 5 ones =

78. In the given picture code each picture stands for a number. Find and write their number in the space given next to their picture.

a.

b.

c.

79. Solve the sums and write the answer in the box. Color as many eggs as the answer of the sums.

a. 8 - 2 =

b. 4 - 1 =

c. 7 - 3 =

d. 5 - 2 =

80. Make your way through the maze by following 1-20.

1	8	7	6	7	8
	2	3	4	5	6	7

1	2	5	12	11	10	9	8
2	3	4	13	16	16	17	18
7	6	5	14	17	15	18	19
12	7	10	15	18	17	19	20
11	8	9	16	19	20		
10	9	18	17	18	20		

81. Color by numbers.

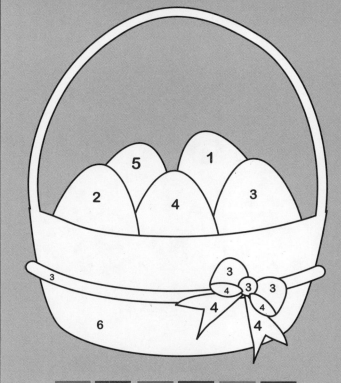

| 1 | 2 | 3 | 4 | 5 | 6 |

33

Subtraction Fun

82. Subtract the colored fruits from the total number of fruits. Write the answer in the given space.

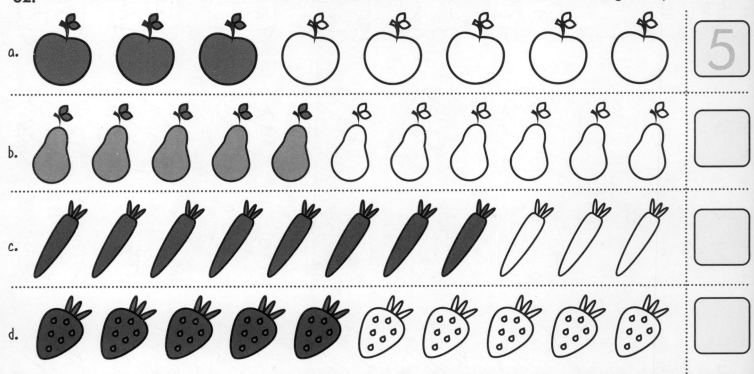

a. | 5

b. |

c. |

d. |

83. Count and write the value of each fruit and then solve the sums.

1. [ ]   2. [ ]   3. [ ]   4. [ ]

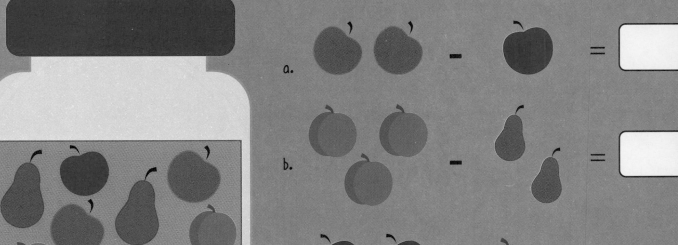

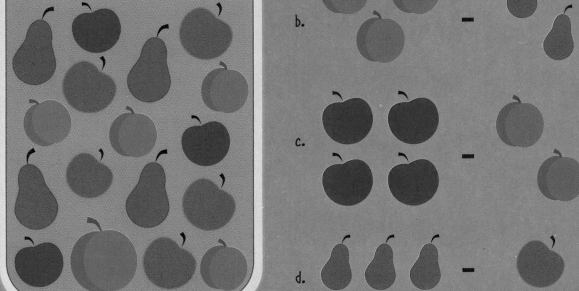

a. ⬤⬤ − ⬤ = [ ]

b. ⬤⬤ − 🍐 = [ ]

c. ⬤⬤⬤⬤ − ⬤ = [ ]

d. 🍐🍐🍐 − ⬤ = [ ]

84. Fill in the missing numbers by subtracting 2 from each tomato.

a. 55 53 ◯ ◯ 47

b. 21 ◯ 17 ◯ 13

c. 72 ◯ ◯ 66 ◯

d. 12 ◯ 8 ◯ 4

85. Solve the sums on the fruit baskets.

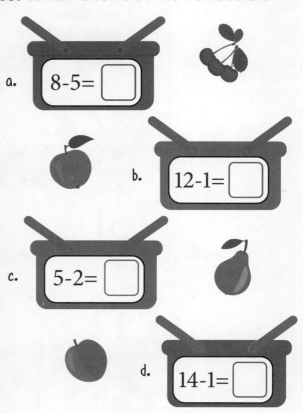

a. 8-5=☐

b. 12-1=☐

c. 5-2=☐

d. 14-1=☐

86. Tick the correct option.

a.
4 - 3 = ☐

b.
3 - 1 = ☐

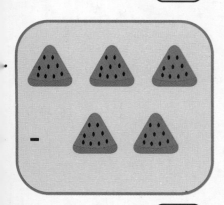
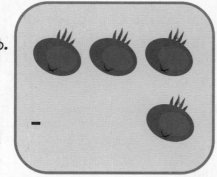

c.
3 - 2 = ☐

d.
4 - 2 = ☐

87. Solve the word problems and write the answers in the box.

a. A shopkeeper sold 29 pears in a week. If he had 40 pears in total, how many pears remain with him?

b. There are 9 potatoes on a table. Rio picks up 2. How many potatoes are left on the table?

c. There are 15 apples in a basket. Mason ate 3 apples. How many apples remain in the basket?

88. Fill in the numbers that come before and after the given numbers.

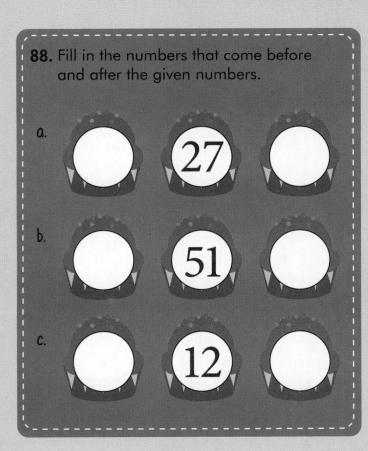

a. ___ 27 ___

b. ___ 51 ___

c. ___ 12 ___

89. Help the first butterfly reach the second butterfly by adding 3 to each flower.

5

32

90. >, < or =?

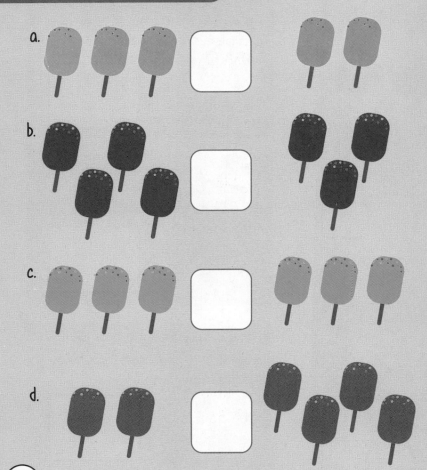

a.

b.

c.

d.

91. Match the following.

a. 9   a. Twelve

b. 6   b. Sixteen

c. 12   c. Nine

d. 16   d. Eighteen

e. 18   e. Six

92. Color by numbers.

- 1
- 2
- 3
- 4

93. Word problems.

a. Lucy baked 5 cupcakes. Then she baked another 4 cupcakes. How many cupcakes did Lucy bake altogether?

Lucy baked [ ] cupcakes altogether.

b. Martha bought 7 ice creams. Then she bought 2 more ice creams. How many ice creams did Martha buy altogether?

Martha bought [ ] ice creams altogether.

94. Study the image and answer the questions.

a. What is the color of the balloons with the highest and lowest count?

_ _

b. Count and write the number of the balloons.

a. _ _ _ _ _ _ _ _ _ _

b. _ _ _ _ _ _ _ _ _ _

c. _ _ _ _ _ _ _ _ _ _

95. Solve and write.

a. $9 - 2 =$

b. $8 - 3 =$

c. $7 - 3 =$

d. $5 - 2 =$

e. $4 - 1 =$

f. $9 - 7 =$

g. $6 - 5 =$

h. $7 - 4 =$

96. Color by numbers.

○ 3-2 ● 6-4 ● 7-5 ● 8-4

97. Write the missing numbers by subtracting 3 each time.

a. 12

b. 54

c. 37

98. Solve the sum, trace the line and write the answer.

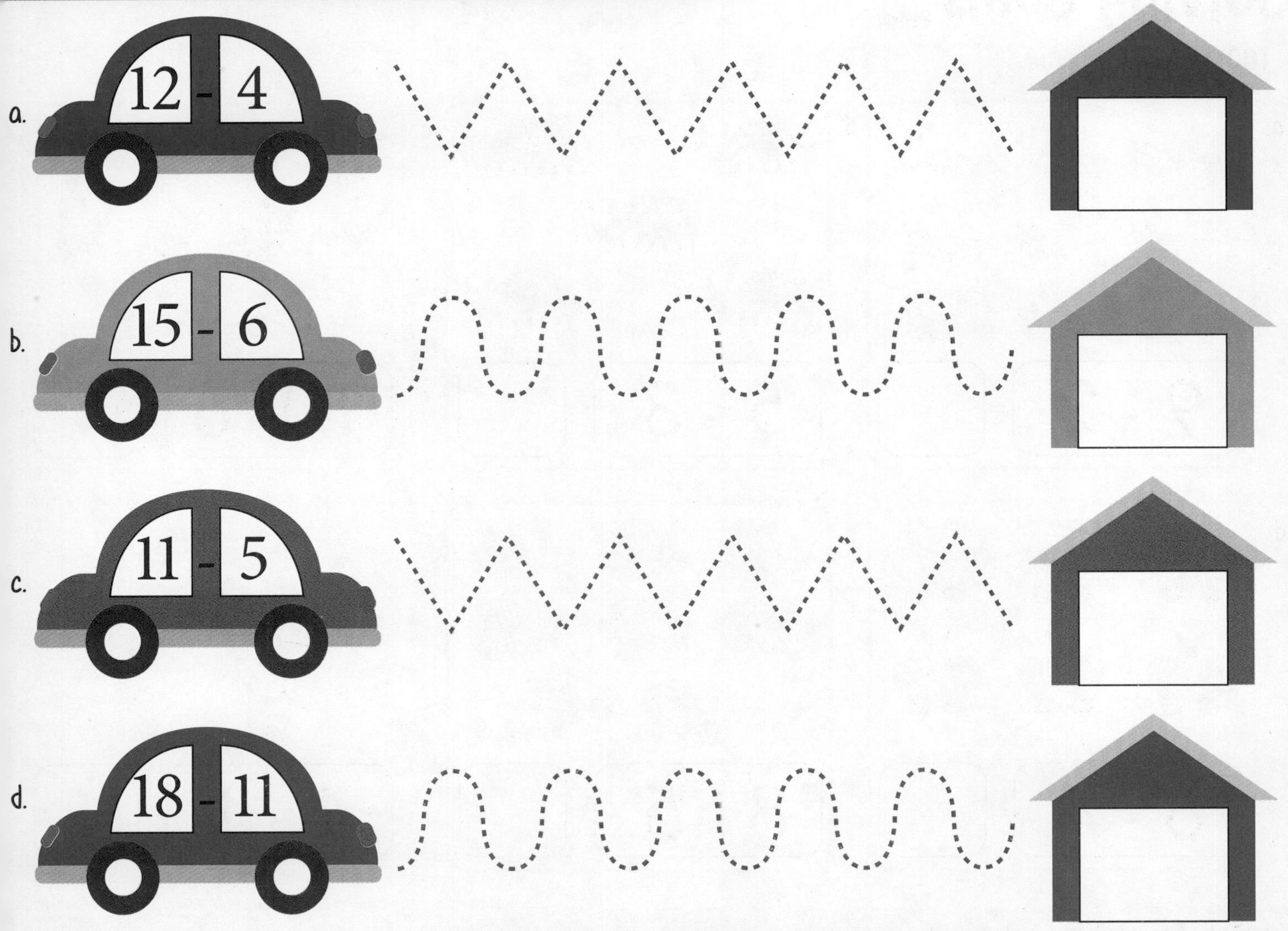

a. 12 - 4

b. 15 - 6

c. 11 - 5

d. 18 - 11

99. Solve and write.

a. 10-5

b. 14-8

c. 12-7

d. 9-3

Solving Sums

100. Solve and write.

a.
$9 - 2$ =

b.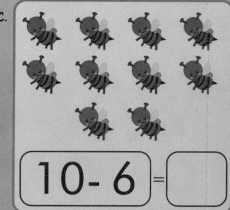
$5 - 3$ =

c.
$10 - 6$ =

d.
$6 - 4$ =

e.
$8 - 5$ =

f.
$4 - 1$ =

101. Subtract 2 in each row to complete the patterns.

a.  6 4

b.  16

c.  12

102. Match the following.

a. $5 - 3$ a. 6

b. $9 - 5$ b. 5

c. $6 - 3$ c. 3

d. $7 - 1$ d. 2

e. $8 - 3$ e. 4

103. Practise addition.

a. 6 + 6 =

b. 8 + 1 =

c. 5 + 7 =

d. 3 + 8 =

104. Solve and write the missing numbers.

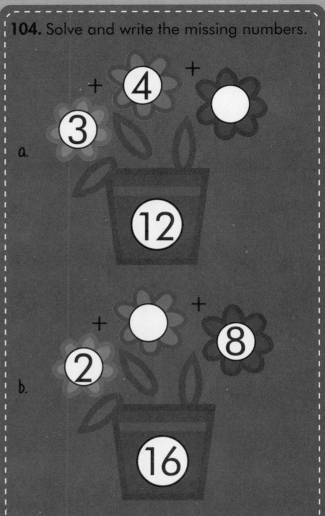

a. + 3 + 4 + = 12

b. 2 + + 8 = 16

105. Solve the sums and help the frog reach the lotus by following the path that goes from 1-10.

7-5   6+3   5+2   9-1   5+5   1+3
8-2   1+4   2+2   6-3
2+3   4-2   5+3   6-3
3-2   9-7   1+8
8-5   5-4

106. Color by numbers.

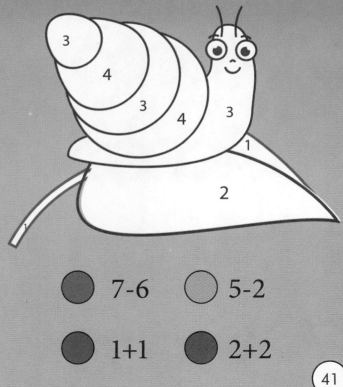

⬤ 7-6   ◯ 5-2

⬤ 1+1   ⬤ 2+2

41

107. Think and write the ordinal number of the colored object.

a. 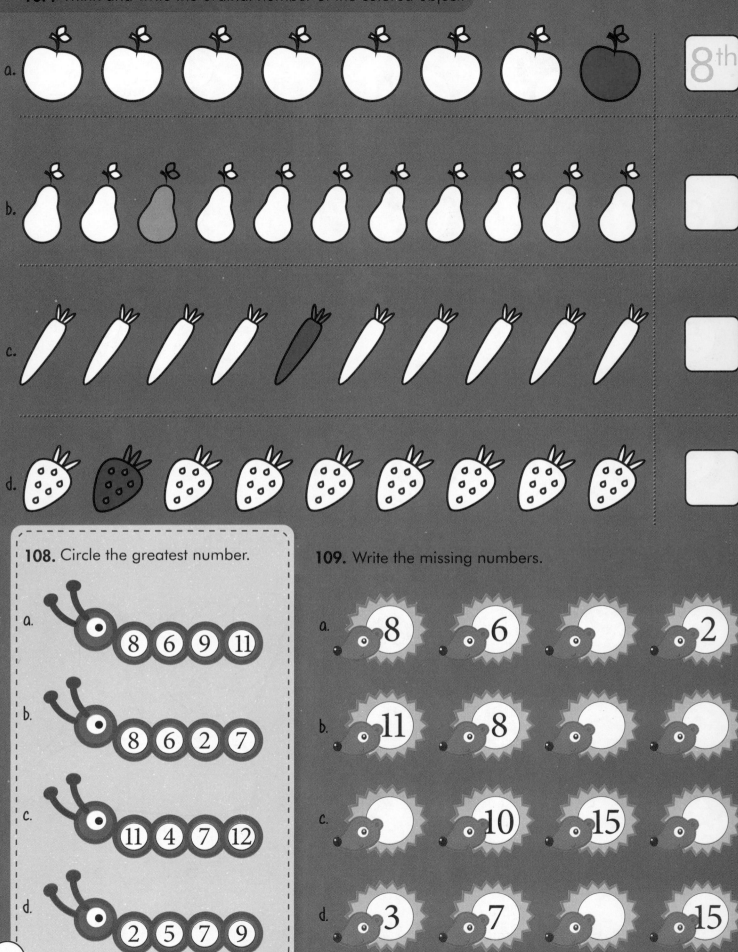 8th

b.

c.

d.

108. Circle the greatest number.

a. 8 6 9 11

b. 8 6 2 7

c. 11 4 7 12

d. 2 5 7 9

109. Write the missing numbers.

a. 8 6 2

b. 11 8

c. 10 15

d. 3 7 15

42

110. Write 2 numbers before and after the given number.

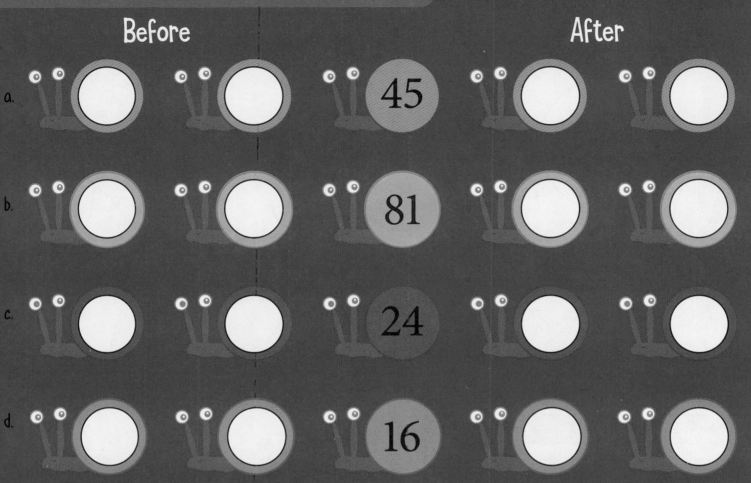

Before		45	After	
a.				
b.		81		
c.		24		
d.		16		

111. Circle the groups of tens. Count the ones. Write the ones and tens. Write the final number in the given space.

a.

_____ tens _____ ones = _____

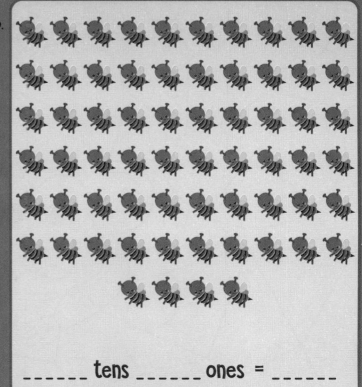

b.

_____ tens _____ ones = _____

43

Color by Number

112. Color by number.

○ 1 ● 2 ○ 3 ○ 4

113. Color the cute fish by number.

○ 1 ● 2 ○ 3 ○ 4

114. Find the hidden animal and color by number.

● 2+1

● 4-2

● 1+3

● 5-4

● 1+4

● 3+3

● 3+4

● 10-2

115. Color the spotted giraffe by number.

1
2
3
4
5
6
7
8
9

116. Color the cuddly bear by number.

1
2
3
4
5
6
7
8
9

117. Color the little elephant by number.

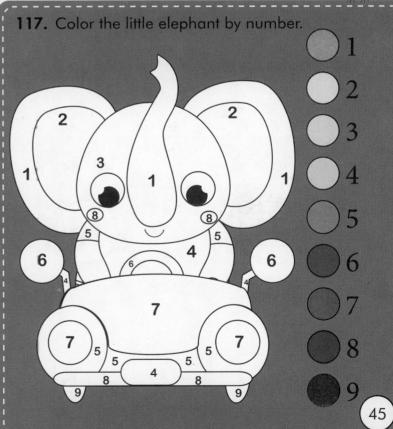

1
2
3
4
5
6
7
8
9

45

118. Mark the boxes with greater than and less than sign. (<,>)

a. 15 ◯ 18

b. 21 ◯ 27

c. 12 ◯ 8

d. 16 ◯ 24

119. Write the place values.

a. 219

_ _ _ _ hundreds + _ _ _ _ tens + _ _ _ _ ones

b. 782

_ _ _ _ hundreds + _ _ _ _ tens + _ _ _ _ ones

c. 451

_ _ _ _ hundreds + _ _ _ _ tens + _ _ _ _ ones

d. 657

_ _ _ _ hundreds + _ _ _ _ tens + _ _ _ _ ones

e. 369

_ _ _ _ hundreds + _ _ _ _ tens + _ _ _ _ ones

120. Match the monsters with the correct answer.

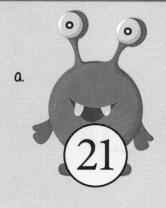
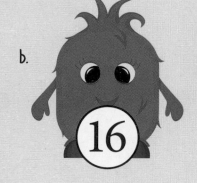

a. 21   b. 16   c. 12   d. 8

a. 10+2   b. 2+6   c. 12+9   d. 8+8

121. Write four more and four less than the number given in the box.

Four less -4					
a.	6	12	14	20	29
Four more +4					

Four less -4					
b.	11	20	44	61	82
Four more +4					

122. Use the value given to each monster and solve the sums.

 3    2   5

a. +  + = ☐

b. + + = ☐

c. + + = ☐

d. + + = ☐

123. Go across the maze by solving the sums and following number 5.

2+2	1+4	4+1	2+3	5+0	←		
3+1	5+0	2+4	5+6	5+4	4+2	2+4	1+3
4+2	3+2	5+1	5+4	6+2	7+2	2+6	1+7
3+3	4+1	1+4	3+6	7+2	2+2	1+3	7+5
5+6	5+4	5+0	2+3	3+2	→		

124. Count the number of cake ingredients and write the answers in the given box.

126. Solve the problems and write the answers in the boxes given below.

a. 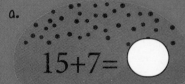 15+7=◯

b.  37-6=◯

c. 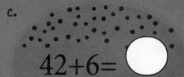 42+6=◯

d. 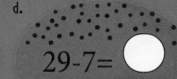 29-7=◯

125. Color the cupcakes as instructed and mark the box with the correct symbol. (<,=,>)

- Greater no. with Red color
- Smaller no. with Yellow color

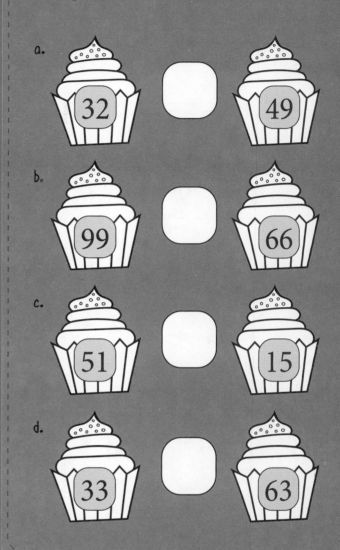

a. 32 ▢ 49

b. 99 ▢ 66

c. 51 ▢ 15

d. 33 ▢ 63

127. The number on each cookie is equal to the sum of two cookies below it. Fill the boxes with the correct number on the cookie pyramid.

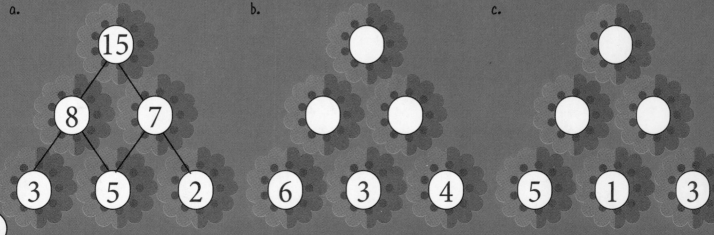

a.
15
8   7
3   5   2

b.
◯
◯   ◯
6   3

c.
◯
◯   ◯
4   5   1   3

128. Add the numbers written on the cupcakes and write the answer in the box given below.

a.

b.

129. Solve the problems and write the missing number.

a.
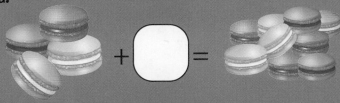 $+$ ☐ $=$

b.
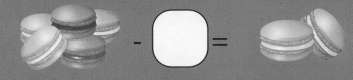 $-$ ☐ $=$

c.
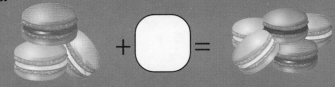 $+$ ☐ $=$

130. Each item has a price. Solve the problems by adding the costs.

a. How much would it cost to buy 1 bread, 2 muffins, 1 cake?

b. How much would it cost to buy 2 bread, 5 muffins?

c. How much would it cost to buy 2 bread, 3 muffins?

d. How much would it cost to buy 2 cakes?

Muffins cost $1 each

Cakes cost $12 each

Bread cost $7 each

131. Add or subtract to answer the given word problems.

a.
You need to buy 8 marshmallows, and you have purchased 3 so far. How many more do you need?

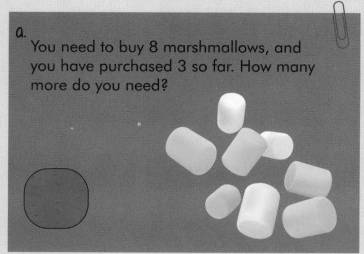

b.
There are 10 candies in a box. If you unwrap 5 candies. How many are left in the box?

c.
There are 4 red-colored candy canes and 5 blue-colored candies. How many are there altogether?

d.
There are 3 candy sticks and 2 chocolate bears. How many are there altogether?

132. Count and mark the candies with the greater than, lesser than sign. (<,=,>)

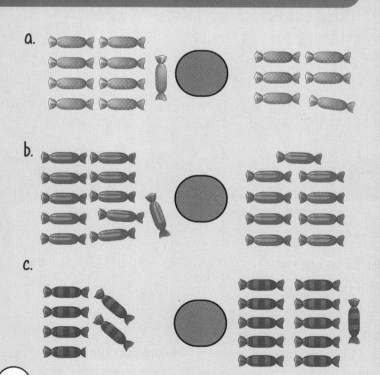

a.

b.

c.

133. Write ten more, ten less than the number given in the box.

Ten less -10					
	21	32	47	50	29
Ten more +10					

Ten less -10					
	11	42	37	89	72
Ten more +10					

50

134. Solve the problems and color the image by the answers gained.

2 = 〰 3 = 〰 4 = 〰 5 = 〰 6 = 〰 7 = 〰 8 = 〰 9 = 〰

135. Count the number of odd and even candies and answer in the space provided.

Odd ◯

Even ◯

136. Solve the picture code puzzle and write the number in the given space.

🍪 8   ⭐ 6   🎄 4   ❄️ 2

a. ⭐ + 🎄 + 🍪 = ▢

b. 🎄 + ❄️ − ⭐ = ▢

c. 🍪 − ⭐ + 🎄 = ▢

137. Connect the dots and color the picture.

138. Count and tally.

a.

b.

c.

d.

139. Count and color the graph accordingly.

140. Solve the sums and match them with their answer.

a. 28   b. 28   c. 22   d. 16   e. 4   f. 35   g. 48   h. 51

1. 10+6   2. 29-7   3. 33-5   4. 17+11   5. 52-4   6. 45+6   7. 11-7   8. 39-4

141. Solve the Christmas pyramid. The number on each ball is equal to the sum of two balls below it.

a.   13   4   9   6

b.   11   22   9

c.   17   12   16

d.   14   16   39

53

142. Fill the addition number spider web. Add the number written in the center with the middle ring number.

a.

19

8 | 13
3 | 6 | 5
15 | 10
3 | 16

b.

3 | 13
5 | 15 | 25
22 | 20
11 | 13

c.

8 | 12
3 | 21 | 4
14 | 16
23 | 6

143. Identify the pattern and find the missing numbers.

a.

___ 8 4 12 ___

b.

6 ___ ___ 15 ___

144. Solve the sums.

12 + 7 = ◯
15 - 5 = ◯
10 + 11 = ◯

145. Count the number of apples and write on the cart. Match the answer with the table of 2.

a.

b.

c.

d.

1. 2 x 2

2. 2 x 4

3. 2 x 3

4. 2 x 6

146. Arrange the numbers written on the pumpkin cart in ascending and descending order on the line.

a.

9 26 15 92 53 31

1. Ascending order

2. Descending order

b.

94 31 20 7 43 13

1. Ascending order

2. Descending order

147. Count and color the graph accordingly.

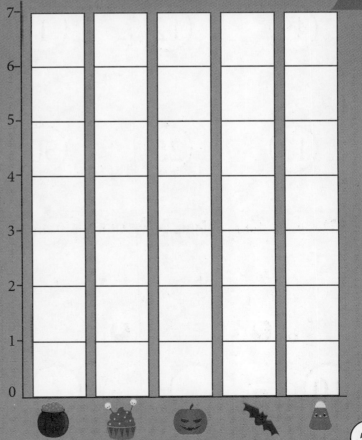

148. Complete the pattern.

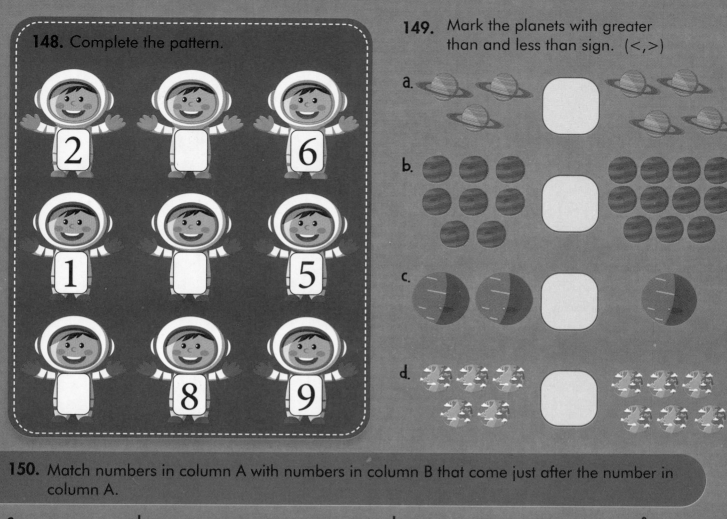

149. Mark the planets with greater than and less than sign. (<,>)

a.

b.

c.

d.

150. Match numbers in column A with numbers in column B that come just after the number in column A.

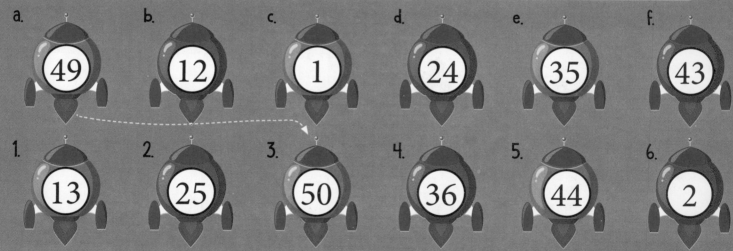

a. 49   b. 12   c. 1   d. 24   e. 35   f. 43

1. 13   2. 25   3. 50   4. 36   5. 44   6. 2

151. Solve the problems from left to right and write the answers in the box next to it.

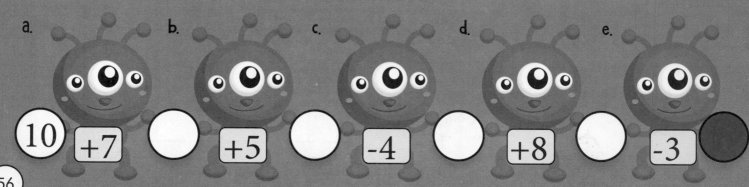

a. 10 +7   b. +5   c. -4   d. +8   e. -3

152. Solve the sums and color according to the instructions.

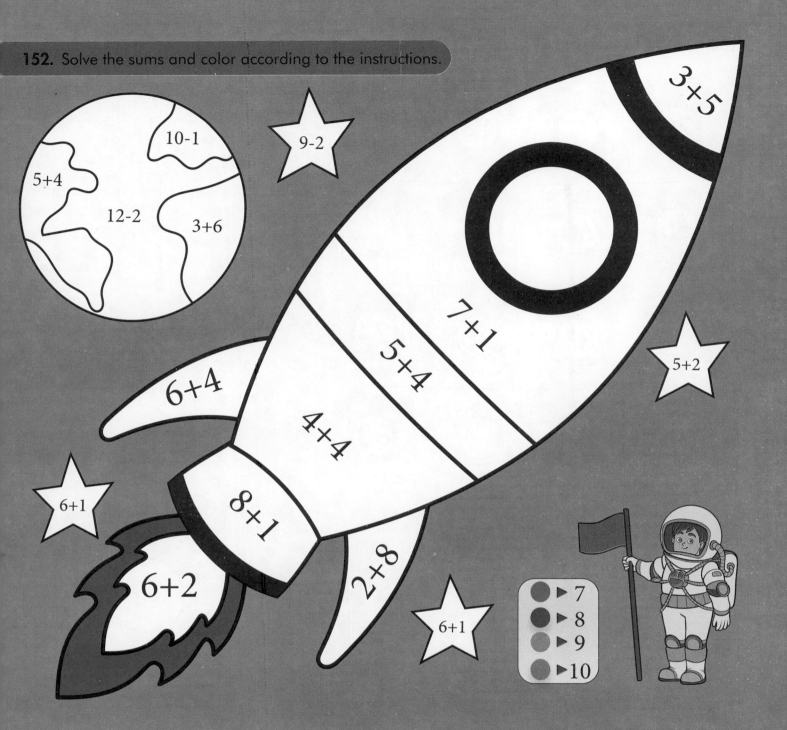

- 3+5
- 10-1
- 9-2
- 5+4
- 12-2
- 3+6
- 7+1
- 5+4
- 5+2
- 6+4
- 4+4
- 6+1
- 8+1
- 2+8
- 6+2
- 6+1

▶ 7
▶ 8
▶ 9
▶ 10

153. Tick the correct answer.

a.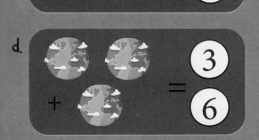
— = 4 / 1

b. — + = 7 / 2

c. — − = 2 / 6

d.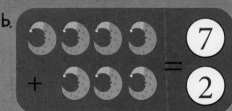
— + = 3 / 6

e.
— + = 7 / 6

f.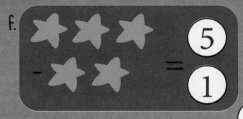
— − = 5 / 1

154. Identify the pattern and write the missing numbers.

a. 20   14   11

b. 65   60   55

c.   36   30   24

d. 86   84   80

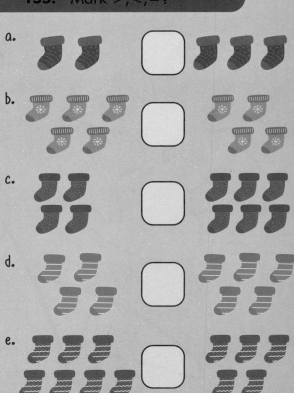

a.

b.

c.

d.

e.

156. Solve the problems and choose the correct option.

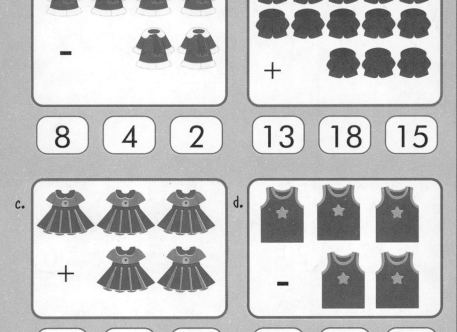

a.   −

b.   +

c.   +

d.   −

8   4   2   13   18   15

4   6   5   1   5   3

157. Solve and color.

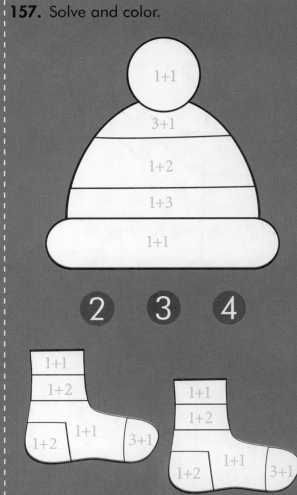

1+1

3+1

1+2

1+3

1+1

2   3   4

1+1
1+2
1+1
1+2   1+1   3+1

1+1
1+2
1+1
1+2   3+1

158. Solve and write.

$10 $3 $12 $20 $25 $20

a. Rocky has $150. He bought pants and a pair of socks. How much change will he get?

b. Mark bought a skirt, a frock and a jacket for his sister. How much did he pay?

c. Nancy has $30. Which two items can she buy?

d. Suzy bought a jacket and a jumper. How much money did she pay altogether?

159. Draw the jumps on the number line and write the answer in the box.

a. 7-2= ☐

1   2   3   4   5   6   7   8

b. 6-4= ☐

1   2   3   4   5   6   7   8

c. 8-5= ☐

1   2   3   4   5   6   7   8

160. Solve and match.

9+5

7+1
1.
2.

6+4
4.

8+4
5.

4+5
3.

3+2
6.

a. 5   b. 12   c. 9   d. 8   e. 10   f. 14

161. Solve and write.

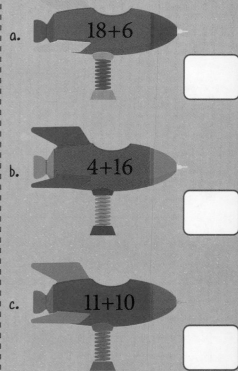

a. 18+6

b. 4+16

c. 11+10

162. Solve the word problems.

a. Eric bought 5 snacks at the fun carnival. He later bought 3 more. How many snacks in total does he have?

b. In the circus carnival, there are 5 elephants, 6 monkeys and 2 lions. How many animals are there in total?

c. Hansel and his 5 friends are eating ice cream. 2 more of his friends join them. Now, how many are eating ice cream in total?

d. Jane bought 6 balloons and her friend Macy bought 8 balloons at the carnival. How many balloons did they buy in total?

163. Count the number of discs and write the answer in the space given on top.

164. Solve the sums using the values written on each ball.

a.

b.

c.

165. Complete and color the pattern.

a.

b.

c.

d.

e.

166. Solve the circus puzzle.

ROAR! 3 +6 +2 +1 +3 +4 +1 +5

167. Add 3 to each balloon.

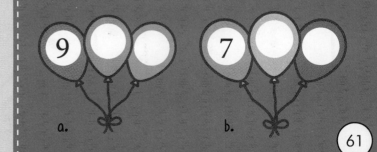

9   7

a.   b.

61

168. Mark the footballs with greater than and less than sign. (<,>)

a. 11 ☐ 19

b. 21 ☐ 15

c. 9 ☐ 6

d. 43 ☐ 39

e. 17 ☐ 27

169. Solve the Sports Balls Suduko puzzle.
Tip - Each row and column should have all the different balls.

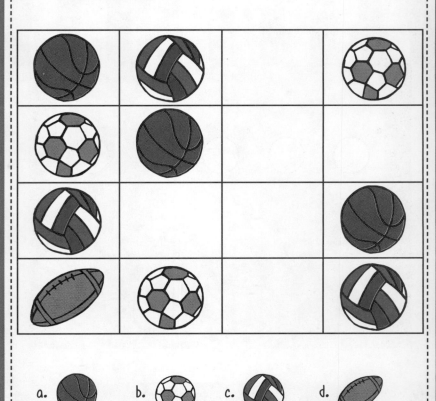

a. ⚫   b. ⚽   c. 🏐   d. 🏈

170. Match the notebook with bags bearing the correct answer.

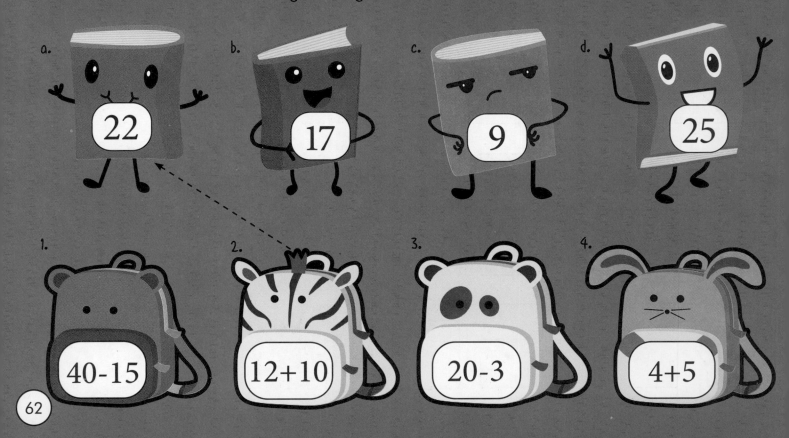

a. 22

b. 17

c. 9

d. 25

1. 40-15

2. 12+10

3. 20-3

4. 4+5

171. Find the total amount that you have to pay
for your purchase.

Colors	_ _ _ _ _
Notebook	_ _ _ _ _
Pencil	_ _ _ _ _

Total ●

Globe	_ _ _ _ _
School Bag	_ _ _ _ _
Sharpener	_ _ _ _ _

Total ●

Clock	_ _ _ _ _
Scissors	_ _ _ _ _
Ball	_ _ _ _ _

Total ●

Colors	_ _ _ _ _
Ball	_ _ _ _ _
Pencil	_ _ _ _ _

Total ●

20
2
30
5
25
15
40
10
50

172. Count the different sports balls, color the graph and mark the tally.

Favorite Sports Bar Graph

Favorite Sports Tally

173. Color the cupcakes with the even numbers.

174. Write the number on the label.

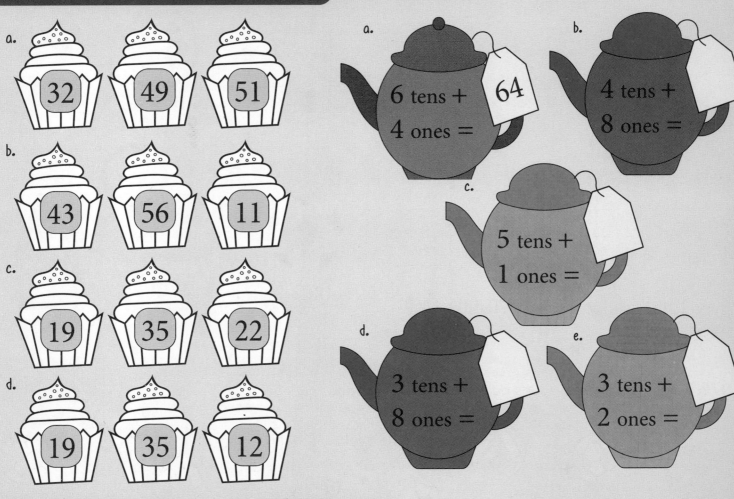

a.

6 tens + 4 ones = 64

b.

4 tens + 8 ones =

c.

5 tens + 1 ones =

d.

3 tens + 8 ones =

e.

3 tens + 2 ones =

a.
32 49 51

b.
43 56 11

c.
19 35 22

d.
19 35 12

175. Count the tens and ones, then write the number.

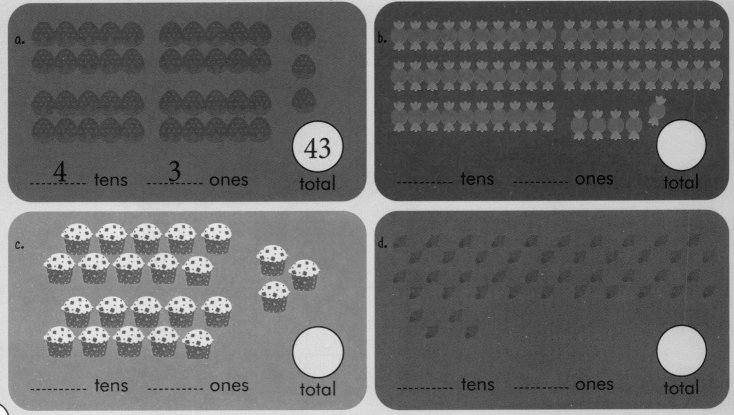

a.
____4____ tens ____3____ ones 43 total

b.
_____ tens _____ ones total

c.
_____ tens _____ ones total

d.
_____ tens _____ ones total

64

176. Add the numbers in the ice cream pyramid. Then place the answer in the tens and ones position in the space below.

a.

9   27

---------- tens ---------- ones

b.

52   11

---------- tens ---------- ones

c.

35   24

---------- tens ---------- ones

177. Answer the questions?

Cupcakes cost $3 each

a. How much would it cost to buy 1 donut, 2 cupcakes and 1 cake?

b. How much would it cost to buy 5 toffees and 2 donuts?

Donuts cost $6 each

Cakes cost $20 each

Toffees cost $1 each

c. How much would it cost to buy 2 macaroons and 1 cake?

d. How much would it cost to buy 2 cakes?

Macaroons cost $5 each

65

178. Solve and reach the maze following 1-10.

179. Tick the correct option.

a.

$\boxed{5}$ $\boxed{9}$ $\boxed{6}$

b.

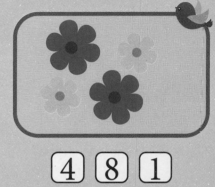

$\boxed{4}$ $\boxed{8}$ $\boxed{1}$

180. Draw the jumps on the number line and write the answer in the box.

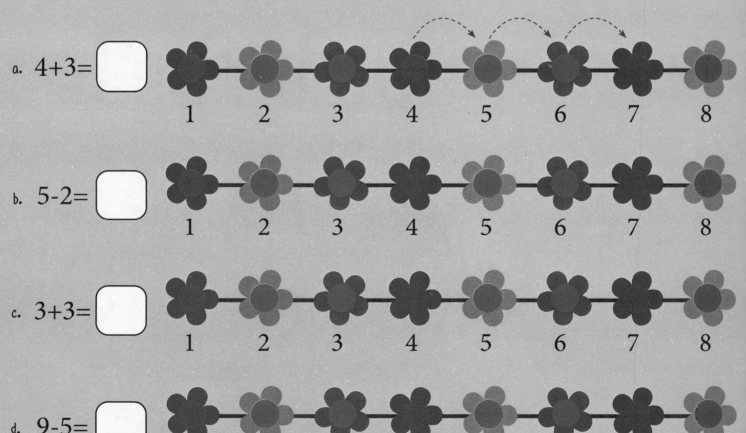

a. 4+3= ☐

1 2 3 4 5 6 7 8

b. 5-2= ☐

1 2 3 4 5 6 7 8

c. 3+3= ☐

1 2 3 4 5 6 7 8

d. 9-5= ☐

1 2 3 4 5 6 7 8

181. Connect the dashes and add all the numbers that come along the way.

a.

b.

c.

182. Write the expanded form of the numbers along with their place values.

a. **561** My expanded form is

_____ + _____ + _____

I have

_____ hundreds _____ tens _____ ones

b. **498** My expanded form is

_____ + _____ + _____

I have

_____ hundreds _____ tens _____ ones

c. **321** My expanded form is

_____ + _____ + _____

I have

_____ hundreds _____ tens _____ ones

183. Solve and write the value of each item.

4 x 8 = ◯

◯ x 6 = 36

2 x ◯ = 12

184. Choose the correct option.

1　6　4

9　5　2

7　3　5

Count my legs.

Count the flowers.

Count my spots.

185. Solve and match the following.

a.  $2 + 2$ — **4**

b. **6**

c. **5**

d. **8**

a.

b.

c.

d.

186. Add the numbers on top and write the answer in the bubble below.

 12 — 4   6 — 16

a. ◯   b. ◯

 7 — 5   9 — 5

c. ◯   d. ◯

187. Color the one with the highest sum.

a.  $1+9$

b. $8+6$

c.  $7+4$

d. $5+8$

188. Solve the maze by matching the given sum to the correct answer.

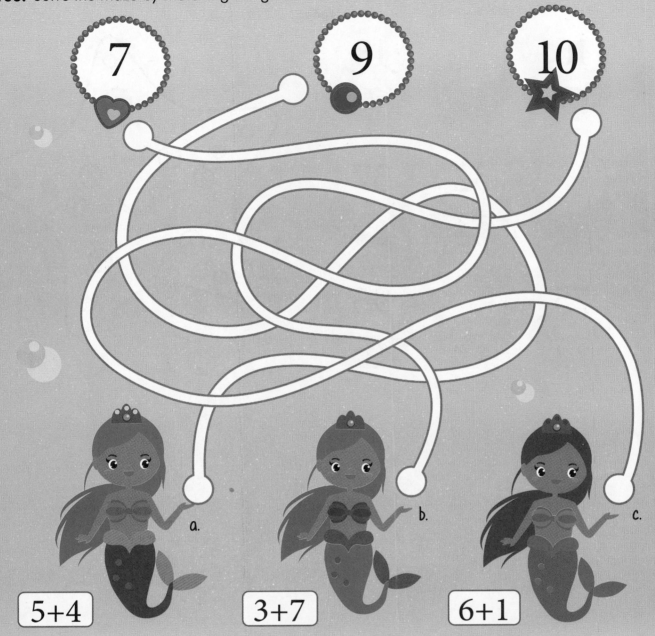

7 9 10

5+4 3+7 6+1

a. b. c.

189. Count and write the value, then solve the sums.

a.   +   =

b.   +   =

c.   +   =

69

190. Fill in the missing numbers.

a. 15   16   ___   18

b. 22   ___   32   37

c. 65   75   ___   95

191. Color by numbers.

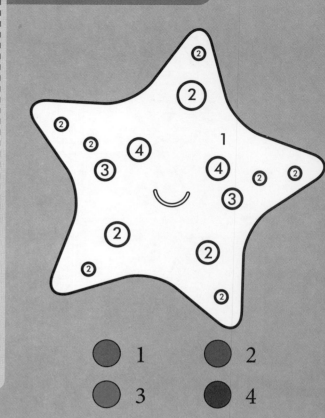

◯ 1   ● 2

◯ 3   ● 4

192. Count and circle the correct number.

a.

| 6 | 3 | 7 |

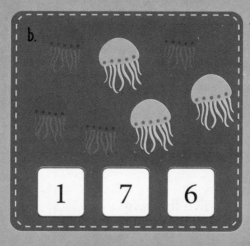

b.

| 1 | 7 | 6 |

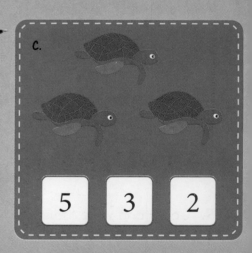

c.

| 5 | 3 | 2 |

d.

| 5 | 6 | 2 |

e.

| 4 | 9 | 7 |

f.

| 4 | 5 | 3 |

70

193. Skip count by 4 and 20 and write the numbers that come after it.

a.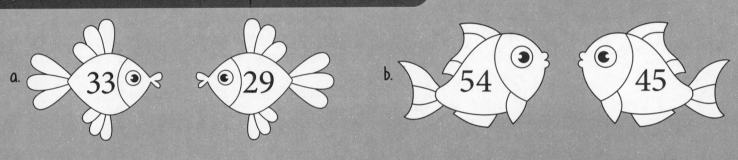

b.

194. Color the ones with the greater number in the group.

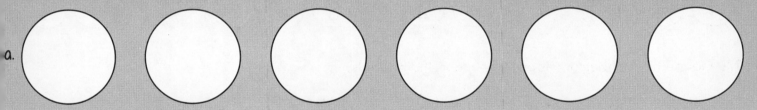

a. 33 29   b. 54 45

195. Color according to the given instructions.

Color the 4th circle pink and the 6th circle blue.

a.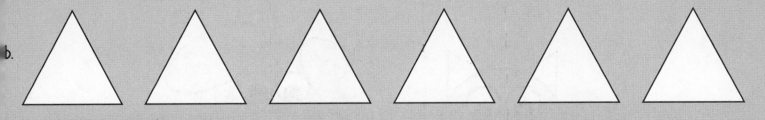

Color the 5th triangle red and the 1st triangle green.

b.

Color the 3rd star yellow and the 2nd star orange.

c.

Fun with Shapes

196. Color and count the sides of each shape and circle the correct number.

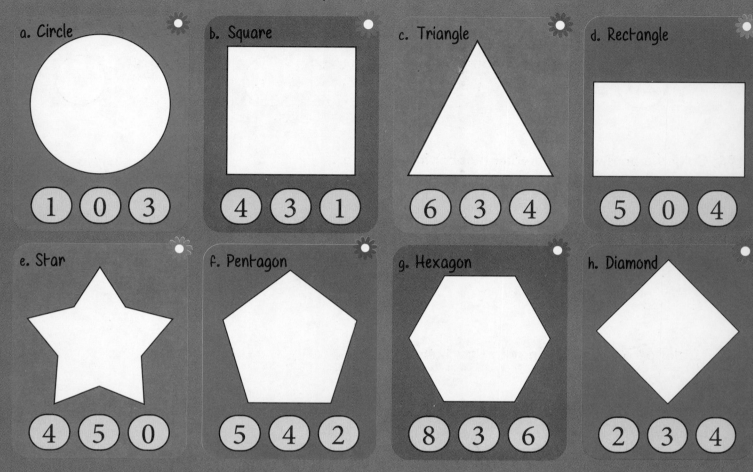

a. Circle — ① ⓪ ③

b. Square — ④ ③ ①

c. Triangle — ⑥ ③ ④

d. Rectangle — ⑤ ⓪ ④

e. Star — ④ ⑤ ⓪

f. Pentagon — ⑤ ④ ②

g. Hexagon — ⑧ ③ ⑥

h. Diamond — ② ③ ④

197. Count the number of shapes you see in the animals.

a.   b.   c.   d.

198. Color the shapes, count them and complete the graph.

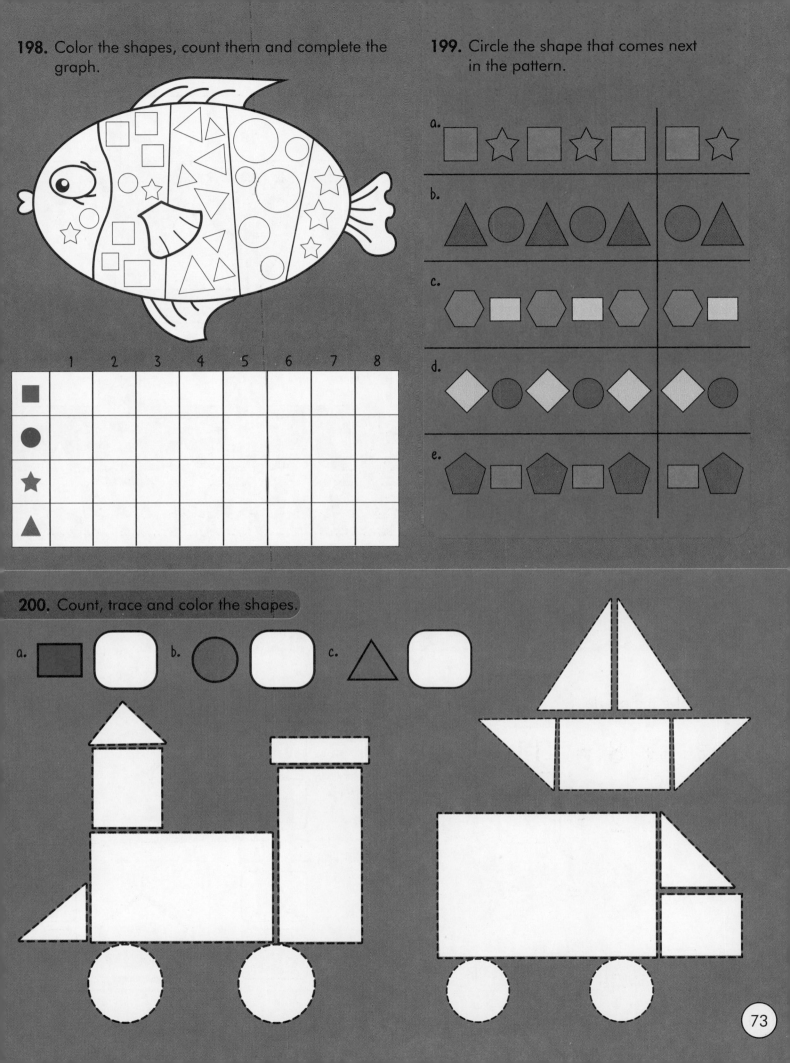

	1	2	3	4	5	6	7	8
■								
●								
★								
▲								

199. Circle the shape that comes next in the pattern.

a.

b.

c.

d.

e.

200. Count, trace and color the shapes.

a.

b.

c.

201. Color the shapes according to the number of their sides.

a.

b.

c.

d.

e.

202. Solve the puzzle.

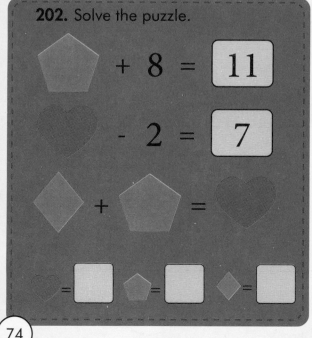

$+ 8 = \boxed{11}$

$- 2 = \boxed{7}$

$\diamond + \pentagon = \heart$

$\heart = \boxed{}$ $\pentagon = \boxed{}$ $\diamond = \boxed{}$

203. Choose the correct option.

a.

b.

c.

d.

204. Count and identify the shapes.

a. Count and write

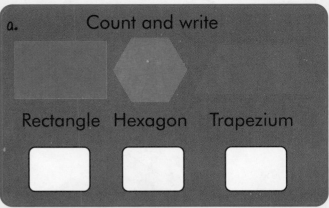

Rectangle   Hexagon   Trapezium

[ ]   [ ]   [ ]

b. Count and write

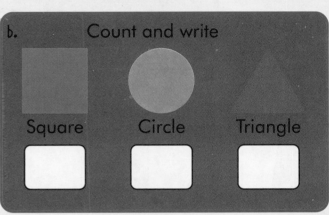

Square   Circle   Triangle

[ ]   [ ]   [ ]

205. Color the shapes and complete the graph.

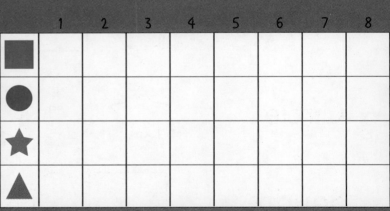

	1	2	3	4	5	6	7	8
■								
●								
★								
▲								

a. Which shape has the highest count?

_ _

b. Which shape has the lowest count?

_ _

206. Count the number of shapes you see in the picture.

a. ⬛ b. 🔵 c. 🔺

⚪ ⚪ ⚪

207. Color the butterfly as per the color code.

208. Find and circle the shape.

a. Triangle

b. Circle

c. Square

d. Rectangle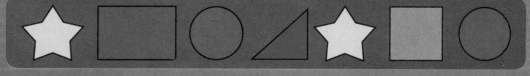

e. Star

209. Match the objects with their shapes.

210. Count the shapes in the Easter egg. Trace and color as per the color code.

a.
b.
c.
d.
e.
f.

211. Count, trace and color the shapes.

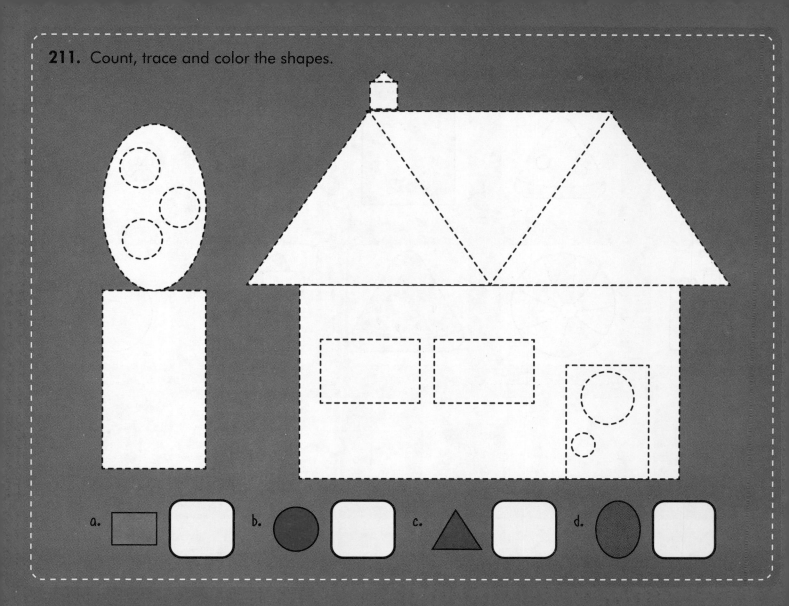

a. ▭ ▢ b. ⬤ ▢ c. ▲ ▢ d. ⬬ ▢

212. Observe the shapes of the given objects and write their number in the box.

a.

b.

c.

213. Answer the following questions.

a. Name and draw a shape with 4 equal sides and 4 equal angles.

_____

b. Name and draw a shape with 5 sides.

_____

c. Name and draw a shape with 3 sides and 3 angles.

_____

d. Name and draw a shape with 6 sides and 6 angles.

_____

e. Name and draw a shape with 8 sides and 8 angles.

_____

f. Name and draw a shape with 4 sides. The opposite sides of this shape have the same length and are parallel.

_____

214. Complete the pattern.

215. Match the following.

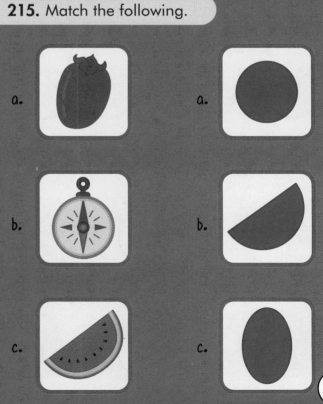

79

216. Help the cute dog reach the ball by following the number maze from 1 - 20.

1	8	7	6	7	8
2	3	4	5	6	7

1	2	5	12	11	10	9	8
2	3	4	13	16	16	17	18
7	6	5	14	17	15	18	19
12	7	10	15	18	17	19	20
11	8	9	16	19	20		
10	9	18	17	18	20		

217. Solve the sums and help the dogs reach their home.

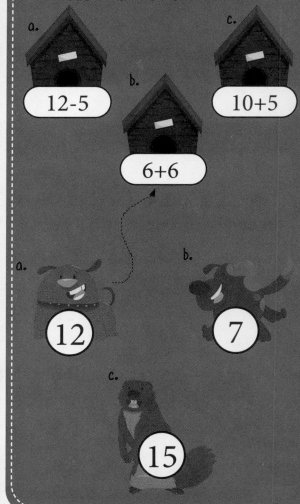

a. 12-5

b. 6+6

c. 10+5

a. 12

b. 7

c. 15

218. Color the bone that has even number as its answer.

a. 11+7= ◯

b. 9+6= ◯

c. 15+8= ◯

219. Identify the pattern and find the missing numbers.

a. Skip count 4.

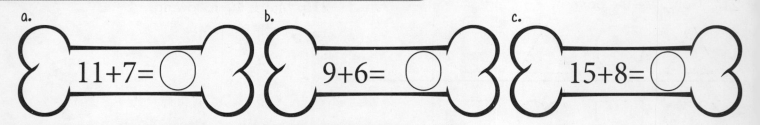

4 | | 12 | | 20 |

b. Skip count 7.

7 | | 21 | | 35 |

220. Solve the picture code puzzle and write the number in the given space.

🏠 10　🔵 2　🪥 4　🥣 5

a. 🏠 + 🥣 + 🔵 = ☐

b. 🥣 + 🪥 − 🔵 = ☐

c. 🏠 − 🥣 + 🪥 = ☐

d. 🪥🔵 − 🥣 + 🪥 = ☐

221. Join the dots and color the dog.

222. How many dogs and cats do you see?

a. Dogs ☐

b. Cats ☐

81

223. Fill in the missing numbers. Count 10's going down and count by 1's going across.

a.

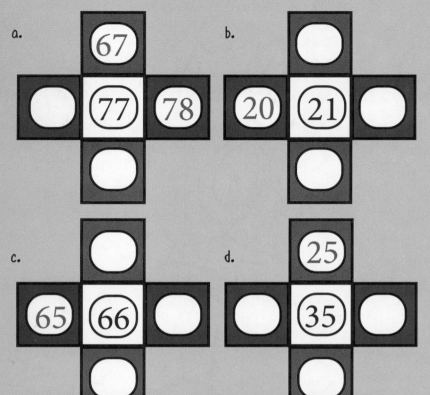

67

77 78

b.

20 21

224. Fill in the box with the addition or subtraction sign.

a. 11 (+) 8 = 19

b. 22 ◯ 5 = 17

c. 11 ◯ 4 = 15

d. 15 ◯ 3 = 12

e. 28 ◯ 7 = 21

c.

65 66

d.

25

35

225. Look at the objects carefully and then answer the questions.

a. How many circle shaped objects can you spot?

b. How many triangle objects can you spot?

c. How many square objects can you spot?

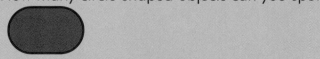

d. How many rectangle objects can you spot?

226. Number bond 20. Fill in the missing place. Tip - Total of the two number will always be 20.

a. 20, 15
b. 20, 11
c. 20, 7
d. 20, 10
e. 20, 17
f. 20, 5

227. Count and tally.

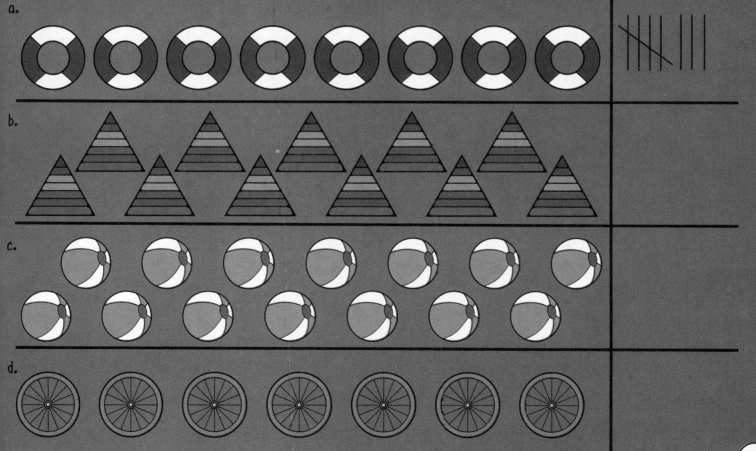

What's the Time?

228. What's the time in the clock?

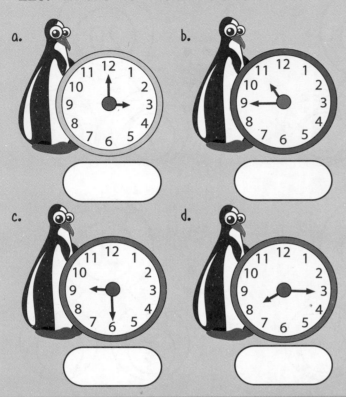

a.

b.

c.

d.

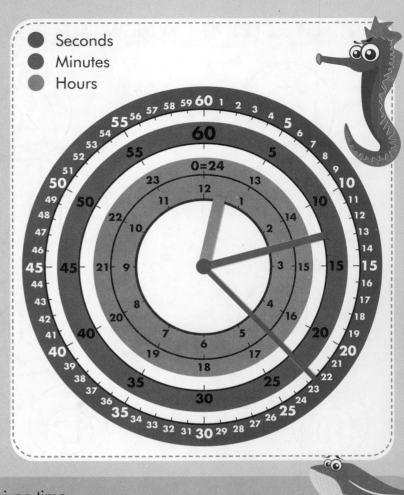

● Seconds
● Minutes
● Hours

229. Draw hands on each clock to mark the given time.

a. 2 :00

b. 5 :30

c. 8 :35

d. 6 :10

e. 11:05

f. 4 :45

230. Draw the hands on the clock to show the time and write the time in the given box.

a. six o' clock

06:00

b. seven o' clock

c. twelve o' clock

d. three o' clock

231. Study the clock and tick the correct answer.

a.

12:45

01:45

05:00

b.

12:15

03:00

05:00

232. Solve the word problems.

a.
I left home at 7 am for school, its a 15 minutes drive from home to school. What time did I reach school?

b.
My swimming class starts at 4 pm and ends at 6 pm. What is the duration of the class?

c.
It takes 1 hour to bake a cake. If I start at 3 pm. What time would I finish baking?

d.
My favorite TV show starts at 6:30 pm. It's a one hour show. What time does it finish?

e.
I sleep at 10:30 pm and wake up at 6:00 am. How many hours do I sleep?

f.
The zoo open at 10 am and closes at 5 pm. How long is the zoo open in a day?

233. What's the time in the clock?

a.

Half past _____

b.

Half past _____

c.

Half past _____

d.

Half past _____

234. Tick the correct option.

a.
- ⭘ 6 o' clock
- ⭘ 8 o' clock
- ⭘ 4 o' clock

b.
- ⭘ 1 o' clock
- ⭘ 3 o' clock
- ⭘ 5 o' clock

c.
- ⭘ 2 o' clock
- ⭘ 9 o' clock
- ⭘ 7 o' clock

d.
- ⭘ 1 o' clock
- ⭘ 2 o' clock
- ⭘ 3 o' clock

235. Match the following.

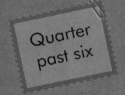 Quarter past six

 Seven O'clock

 Quarter to three

 Half past ten

a.

b.

c.

d.

 **7:00**

 **2:45**

 **6:15**

10:30

236. Draw hands on the clocks.

a.

4 o'clock

b.

Quarter past nine

c.

Half past seven

d.

Quarter to one

237. First write the time in 'Now' column as shown in the clock. Then write the time in 'Earlier' and 'Later' columns.

One hour earlier	Now	One hour later
a.		
b.		
c.		
d.		

238. What's the time in the clock?

a. Quarter past _____

_____

b. Quarter past _____

_____

c. Quarter past _____

_____

d. Quarter past _____

_____

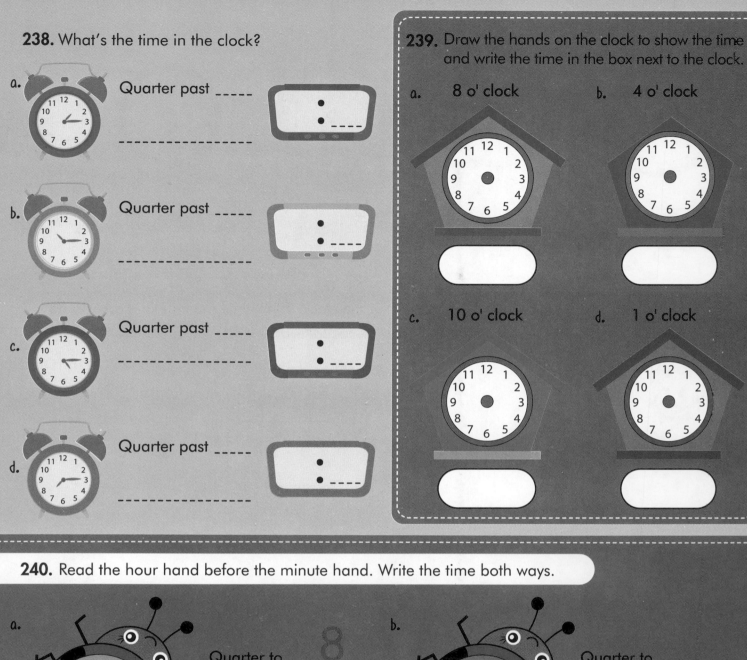

239. Draw the hands on the clock to show the time and write the time in the box next to the clock.

a. 8 o' clock

b. 4 o' clock

c. 10 o' clock

d. 1 o' clock

240. Read the hour hand before the minute hand. Write the time both ways.

a. Quarter to __8__

__7:45__

b. Quarter to _____

_____

c. Quarter to _____

_____

d. Quarter to _____

_____

241. Draw the minute and hour hands and write the time of your daily routine.

a. I wake up at

b. I take a bath at

c. I eat breakfast at

d. I go to school at

e. I eat lunch at

f. I do my homework at

g. I play at

h. I eat dinner at

i. I sleep at

242. How many minutes are shown in the colored part of the clock?

a.

b.

c.

d.
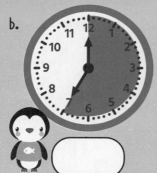

243. Word problems.

a.
Amy went to the park with Mary at 4 pm. They played for 3 hours. At what time did they stop playing?
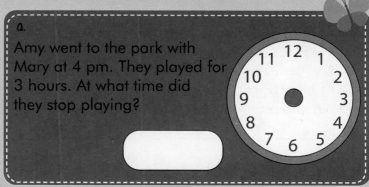

b.
Jake finished watching his favorite show. The show is 2 hours long and now its 7 pm. At what time did the show start?

244. Draw the hands to tell the starting time.

End Time   Start Time

a.

4:00

Game is **3** hours long.

b.

7:00

The movie is **2** hours long.

c.

01:30

Lunch time is **30** minutes long.

d.

12:45

The trip to the zoo is **2** hours long.

245. Write the time.

a.

b.

c.

d.

e.

f.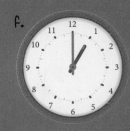

246. Solve the given word problems.

a.
Tara goes to the pool at 2 pm. She swims for an hour and 25 minutes, then she walks home. It takes her 10 minutes. What time did she return home?

b.
Jerry goes to the beach at 3 o'clock, and he makes 5 sand castles. It took him 20 minutes to create each sand castle. What time was he done?

c.
Becky is meeting her friend at the library at 12:45 pm. It takes her 25 minutes to get to the library. What time will she need to leave her house to reach on time?

d.
Ethan's birthday party started at 4:30 pm. The last guest left at 6:32 pm. How long did Ethan's party last?

e.
Dad arrives home at 4:50 pm. He left work 40 minutes ago. What time did Dad get off work?

f.
Jordan got to football practice at 7:05 pm. Steve showed up 11 minutes later. What time did Steve get to practice?

247. Draw hands on the clocks as instructed.

a.

b.

c.

d.

248. Read carefully and write the answers.

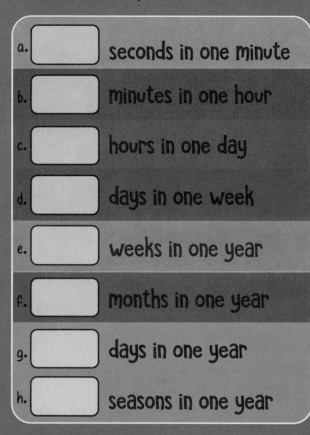

a. [ ] seconds in one minute

b. [ ] minutes in one hour

c. [ ] hours in one day

d. [ ] days in one week

e. [ ] weeks in one year

f. [ ] months in one year

g. [ ] days in one year

h. [ ] seasons in one year

249. Place the hours and minutes in their correct place by drawing a line between them.

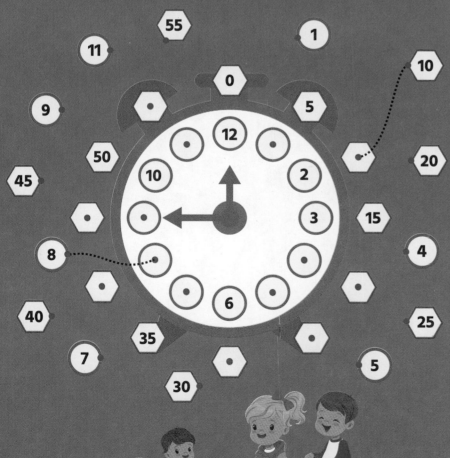

250. Can you tell the time?

a.

b.

c.

d.

e.

f.

251. Multiply and complete the spider web.

a.

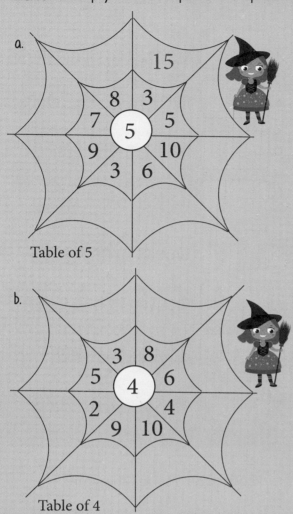

Table of 5

b.

Table of 4

252. Write the place value of the marked digit on the dotted line.

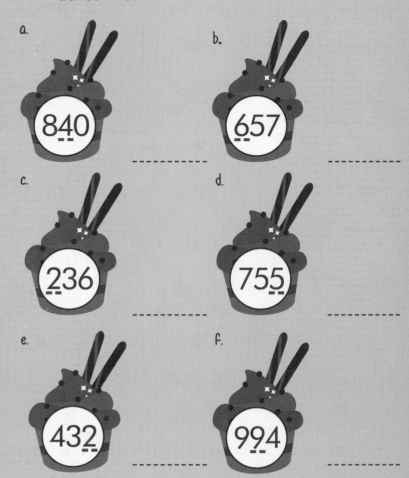

a. 840 ----------

b. 657 ----------

c. 236 ----------

d. 755 ----------

e. 432 ----------

f. 994 ----------

253. Solve and write.

 2 4 6

a.
x
6 x 6 =

b.
x
=

c.
x
=

d.
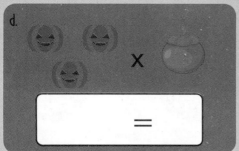
x
=

e.
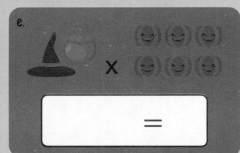
x
=

f.

x
=

254. Solve the sums.

$$9 + \bigcirc = 14$$
$$- \quad + \quad -$$
$$\bigcirc - 5 = \bigcirc$$
$$= \quad = \quad =$$
$$\bigcirc + \bigcirc = 12$$

255. Solve the word problems.

a.

Jane sees 7 cats and her brother Eric sees 5 cats while wandering in the woods. How many cats do they see in all?

b.

Leah receives 15 candies in her trick or treat bag. Max eats 6 of them. How many candies are left in the bag?

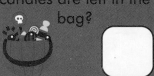

c.

There are 20 children in halloween parade. 12 of them wave flags and the rest sing songs. How many are singing?

d.

If Paul turns into a vampire at midnight and its 5 am right now. How many hours does he remain a vampire?

256. Multiply the number of dots on the dice with the number of dice to answer the problem.

a.

___5___ X ___3___ = ___15___

b.

_____ X _____ = _____

c.

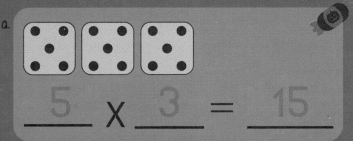

_____ X _____ = _____

d.

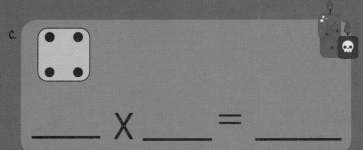

_____ X _____ = _____

e.

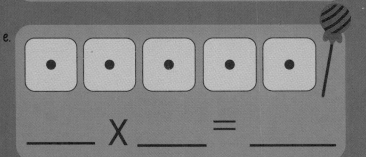

_____ X _____ = _____

f.

_____ X _____ = _____

257. Solve the problem.

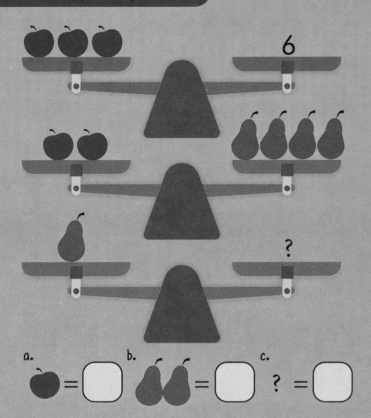

a.  = ☐ b. = ☐ c. ? = ☐

259. Count and write the value of each fruit and then solve the sums.

= ☐   = ☐   = ☐   = ☐

a. + + = ☐

b. + + = ☐

c. + + = ☐

d. + + = ☐

e. + + = ☐

94

260. Write the missing numbers.

a. 15 ◯ ◯ 45 55

b. ◯ 14 21 ◯ 35

c. 9 ◯ 27 36 ◯

d. 12 ◯ 20 ◯ 28

261. Answer the following questions using ordinal numbers.

If the rose is the first flower...

| Rose |
| Sunflower |
| Lily |
| Daisy |
| Tulip |
| Lotus |

a. Which flower is third?

_____

b. Color of the second flower.

_____

c. What place is the tulip in?

_____

d. Which flower is sixth?

_____

262. Tick the correct option.

a. ✳ ✳ ✳ ✳ ✳ ✳ ✳

4 7 1

b.

3 8 11

c.

5 8 3

d.

7 3 2

263. Solve the word problems and write answers in the box.

a. A shopkeeper sold 296 pears in a week and 173 pears in the next week. How many pears did he sell?

b. There are 9 potatoes and 1 pumpkin on a table. How many vegetables are there?

c. There are 283 apples and 317 oranges in a basket. How many fruits were there in the basket?

Graph Fun

264. Count the number of each fish and color the bar graph accordingly. Then answer the questions.

a. How many of each?

b. Which fish appears the most?

_ _

c. Which fish appears the least?

_ _

265. Count and tally.

a.

b.

c.

d.

Which animal has the highest count and by how much?

_ _

266. In a survey, kids liked crabs the most followed by starfish, jellyfish and whale respectively.

a. Write the percentage of each animal.

25%

50%

15%

10%

b. Color the crab-red, whale-blue, starfish-green and jellyfish-pink.

c. If the total number of animals is 200 then find out the number of jellyfish.

_ _ _ _ _ _ _ _ _ _ _ _ _ _ _ _

d. If the total number of animals is 200 then find out the number of starfish and whales together. _ _ _ _ _ _ _ _ _

---

267. Study the graph and answer the questions.

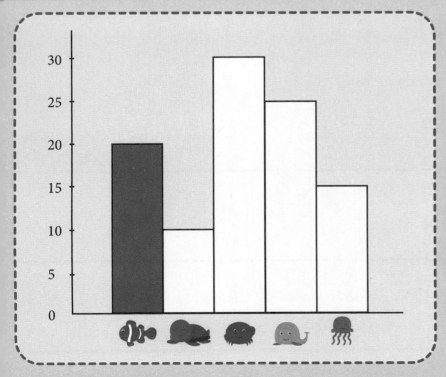

a. How many of each?

20

Solve and write.

a. 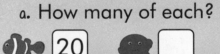 + + =

b. + + =

c. + + =

d. + + =

e.  + + =

Color the following.

Fraction Fun

268. Write the fraction to tell the colored part.

a. $\dfrac{1}{4}$

b. $\dfrac{}{}$

c. $\dfrac{}{}$

d. $\dfrac{}{}$

269. Circle the pirate animals as per the fraction.

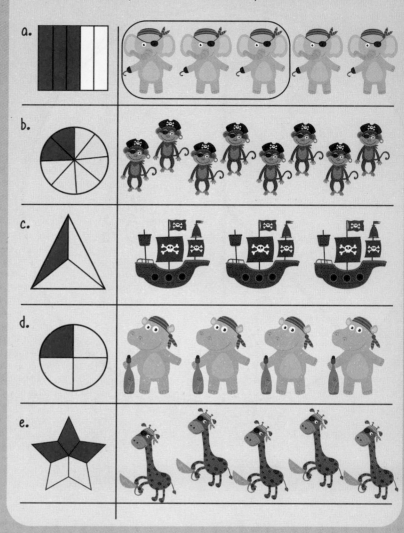

a.

b.

c.

d.

e.

270. Color the objects as per the fraction written in front.

a. $\dfrac{2}{7}$

b. $\dfrac{5}{9}$

c. $\dfrac{3}{8}$

d. $\dfrac{3}{5}$

271. Circle the right answer.

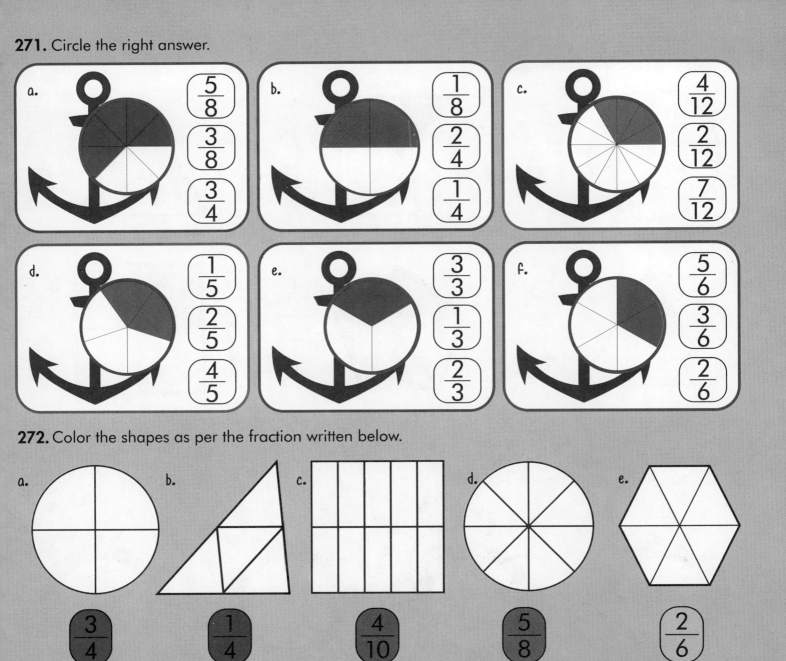

a.
$\frac{5}{8}$
$\frac{3}{8}$
$\frac{3}{4}$

b.
$\frac{1}{8}$
$\frac{2}{4}$
$\frac{1}{4}$

c.
$\frac{4}{12}$
$\frac{2}{12}$
$\frac{7}{12}$

d.
$\frac{1}{5}$
$\frac{2}{5}$
$\frac{4}{5}$

e.
$\frac{3}{3}$
$\frac{1}{3}$
$\frac{2}{3}$

f.
$\frac{5}{6}$
$\frac{3}{6}$
$\frac{2}{6}$

272. Color the shapes as per the fraction written below.

a.   b.   c.   d.   e.

$\frac{3}{4}$ $\frac{1}{4}$ $\frac{4}{10}$ $\frac{5}{8}$ $\frac{2}{6}$

273. Compare the fractions and mark greater than or less than sign (<, >, =).

a.   <

b.

c.

d.

274. Choose the correct fraction.

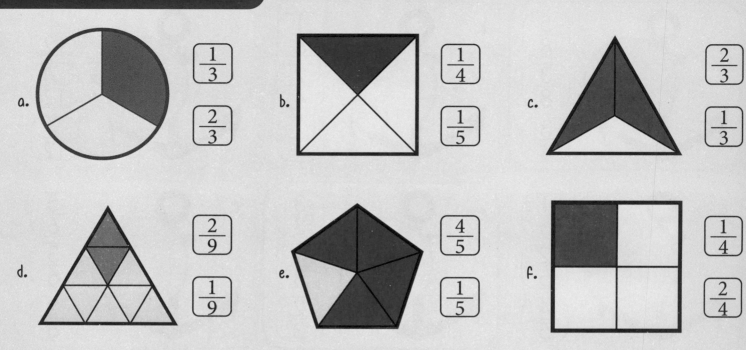

a. $\frac{1}{3}$ $\frac{2}{3}$

b. $\frac{1}{4}$ $\frac{1}{5}$

c. $\frac{2}{3}$ $\frac{1}{3}$

d. $\frac{2}{9}$ $\frac{1}{9}$

e. $\frac{4}{5}$ $\frac{1}{5}$

f. $\frac{1}{4}$ $\frac{2}{4}$

275. Color the buggy fractions as shown.

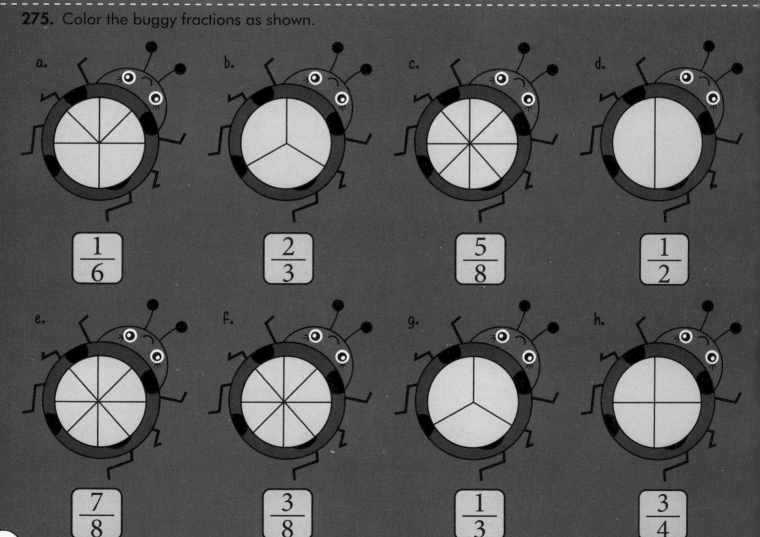

a. $\frac{1}{6}$

b. $\frac{2}{3}$

c. $\frac{5}{8}$

d. $\frac{1}{2}$

e. $\frac{7}{8}$

f. $\frac{3}{8}$

g. $\frac{1}{3}$

h. $\frac{3}{4}$

276. Write fractions of the colored part.

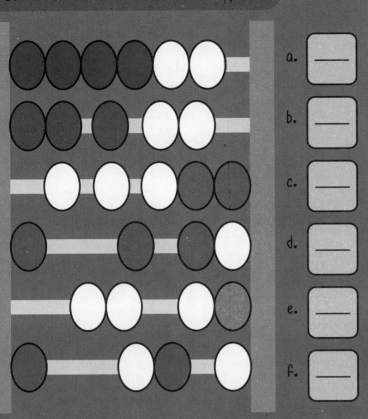

a. ___

b. ___

c. ___

d. ___

e. ___

f. ___

277. Solve the word problems.

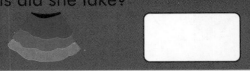
a. There are 10 skirts on the rack. Gilly took 3. What fraction of the skirts did she take?

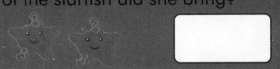

b. Jane saw 7 starfish and brought 2 home with her. What fraction of the starfish did she bring?

c. Out of 12 tomatoes, Mike ate 5 tomatoes. What is the fraction of tomatoes that Mike ate?

278. First, solve the fraction sums and write the answer. Then, color the stacked objects.

a.
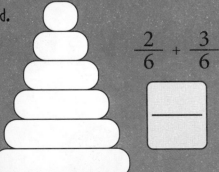
$$\frac{1}{6} + \frac{2}{6}$$
___

b.
$$\frac{4}{6} - \frac{1}{6}$$
___

c.
$$\frac{5}{6} - \frac{1}{6}$$
___

d.
$$\frac{2}{6} + \frac{3}{6}$$
___

e.
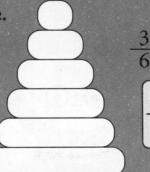
$$\frac{3}{6} + \frac{1}{6}$$
___

f.

$$\frac{2}{6} - \frac{1}{6}$$
___

279. Choose the correct answer.

a. 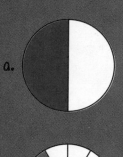 $\dfrac{5}{8}$ a. $\dfrac{1}{2}$ b. $\dfrac{4}{3}$ c.

d.  $\dfrac{9}{2}$ a. $\dfrac{1}{3}$ b. $\dfrac{6}{8}$ c.

b.  $\dfrac{4}{12}$ a. $\dfrac{13}{5}$ b. $\dfrac{3}{8}$ c.

e.  $\dfrac{5}{8}$ a. $\dfrac{5}{6}$ b. $\dfrac{4}{6}$ c.

c. $\dfrac{4}{8}$ a. $\dfrac{5}{8}$ b. $\dfrac{6}{8}$ c.

f. $\dfrac{4}{7}$ a. $\dfrac{5}{7}$ b. $\dfrac{1}{7}$ c.

280. Simplify the fractions given on the tree, then match the following.

On the tree:
$\dfrac{16}{10}$ $\dfrac{9}{6}$ $\dfrac{4}{6}$ $\dfrac{2}{6}$ $\dfrac{20}{12}$ $\dfrac{8}{14}$ $\dfrac{14}{35}$ $\dfrac{5}{10}$ $\dfrac{10}{2}$ $\dfrac{5}{5}$

Options:
a. $\dfrac{2}{3}$ b. $\dfrac{3}{2}$ c. $\dfrac{4}{7}$

d. $\dfrac{2}{5}$ e. $\dfrac{1}{3}$ f. $\dfrac{8}{5}$

g. $\dfrac{1}{2}$ h. 1 i. $\dfrac{5}{3}$

j. $\dfrac{8}{16}$ k. 5

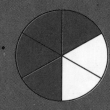

281. Color the circle as shown in the bar. Write the fraction in the given space.

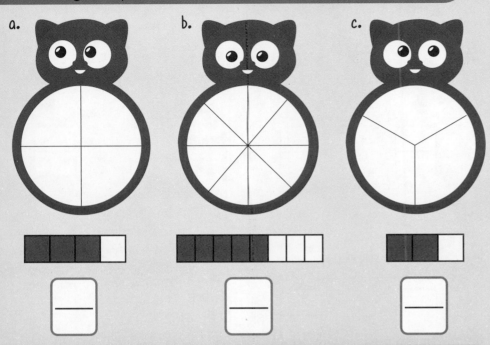

a.   b.   c.

282. Write the fraction for the colored part of the fruit seeds.

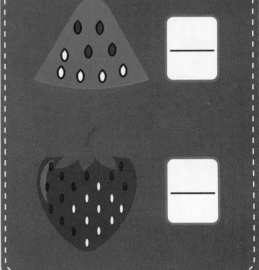

283. Write the fractions.

a.   b.   c.

d.   e.   f.

284. >,< or =?

a. $\dfrac{1}{2}$ ☐ $\dfrac{1}{3}$

b. $\dfrac{4}{12}$ ☐ $\dfrac{5}{12}$

c. $\dfrac{3}{4}$ ☐ $\dfrac{1}{4}$

d. $\dfrac{2}{3}$ ☐ $\dfrac{1}{3}$

e. $\dfrac{1}{2}$ ☐ $\dfrac{3}{4}$

f. $\dfrac{2}{4}$ ☐ $\dfrac{2}{5}$

285. Look at the image and write the fractions.

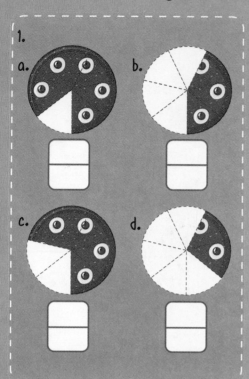

1.
a.
b.
c.
d.

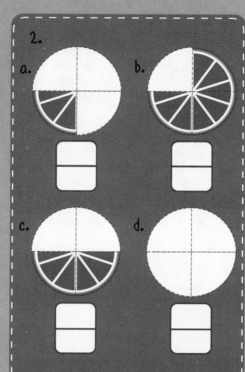

2.
a.
b.
c.
d.

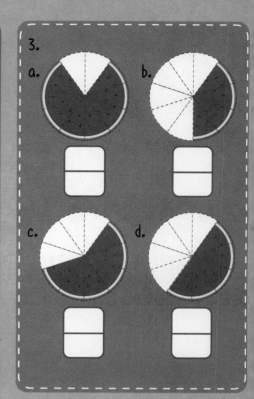

3.
a.
b.
c.
d.

286. Add the fraction and color the answer in the provided space.

a.

b.
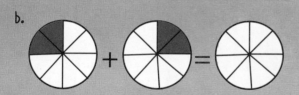

c.
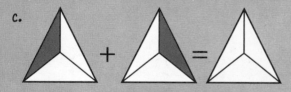

d.
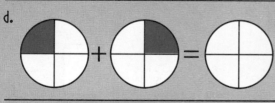

e.
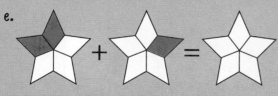

287. Simplify the fraction written on the butterfly and match with the correct option.

a. $\dfrac{4}{16}$ b. $\dfrac{6}{12}$ c. $\dfrac{6}{18}$ d. $\dfrac{5}{15}$ e. $\dfrac{2}{8}$

f. $\dfrac{3}{6}$ g. $\dfrac{5}{10}$ h. $\dfrac{7}{14}$ i. $\dfrac{8}{16}$ j. $\dfrac{2}{4}$

k. $\dfrac{4}{8}$ l. $\dfrac{4}{12}$ m. $\dfrac{2}{6}$ n. $\dfrac{3}{9}$ o. $\dfrac{2}{6}$

2. $\dfrac{1}{3}$

1. $\dfrac{1}{4}$

3. $\dfrac{1}{2}$

288. Color the given fractions as instructed.

a. $\dfrac{2}{4}$

b. $\dfrac{5}{6}$

c. $\dfrac{5}{8}$

d. $\dfrac{7}{10}$

289. Choose the correct option.

a. $\dfrac{2}{6}$ $\dfrac{5}{6}$ $\dfrac{3}{6}$

b. $\dfrac{4}{7}$ $\dfrac{2}{7}$ $\dfrac{1}{7}$

c. $\dfrac{1}{4}$ $\dfrac{2}{4}$ $\dfrac{3}{4}$

290. Write the fraction and choose which is >, <, =.

a.

b.

c.

d.

e.

f.

291. Match the following.

a.

b.

c.

d.

$\dfrac{3}{8}$

$\dfrac{1}{8}$

$\dfrac{1}{4}$

$\dfrac{4}{9}$

$\dfrac{2}{8}$

$\dfrac{3}{16}$

$\dfrac{2}{4}$

$\dfrac{2}{6}$

e.

f.

g.

h.

105

Fruity Fraction

292. Color the fruits according to the given fraction.

a. $\dfrac{5}{7}$

b. $\dfrac{2}{5}$

c. $\dfrac{4}{6}$

d. $\dfrac{1}{5}$

e. $\dfrac{3}{7}$

293. Write the fraction of the colored part of the oranges.

a.   b.   c.   d.

294. Solve the sums and write the answers.

a. 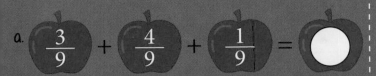 $\frac{3}{9}$ + $\frac{4}{9}$ + $\frac{1}{9}$ = ◯

b. $\frac{1}{5}$ + $\frac{1}{5}$ + $\frac{2}{5}$ = ◯

c. $\frac{3}{7}$ + $\frac{1}{7}$ + $\frac{2}{7}$ = ◯

295. Word problems.

a. Lionel bought 10 fruits. 2/5 of the fruits were apples. How many apples did he buy?

b. Macy had 18 oranges. She gave 1/3 of the oranges to Max. How many oranges Macy gave to Max?

296. Color the boxes according to the fraction given on the fruits.

a.  $\frac{5}{10}$

b. 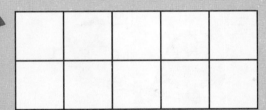 $\frac{4}{10}$

c.  $\frac{6}{10}$

d.  $\frac{1}{10}$

e.  $\frac{3}{10}$

f. 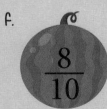 $\frac{8}{10}$

g. $\frac{7}{10}$

h. $\frac{2}{10}$

Measuring Fun

297. Solve. (*1km = 1000m)

a. 5 km + 2 km = [ ] m

b. 9 km + 400 m = [ ] m

c. 2500 m + 100 m = [ ] m

d. 1.5 km + 200 m = [ ] m

e. 3 km + 400 m = [ ] m

298. Order from 1-8 in ascending order (short to long).

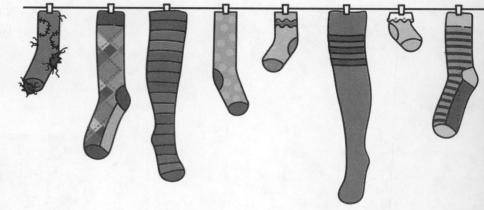

a. [ ] b. [ ] c. [ ] d. [ ] e. [ ] f. [ ] g. [ ] h. [ ]

299. Choose which is heavier?

a.
5kg   100g
A   B

b.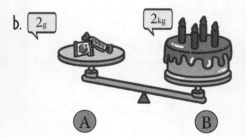
2g   2kg
A   B

c.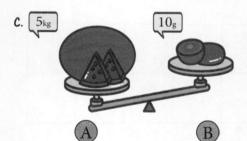
5kg   10g
A   B

d.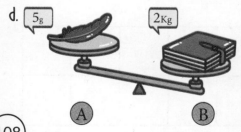
5g   2Kg
A   B

300. Color the blocks to measure the height of each object. Write the number in the circle.

a. ( )
| 10 |
| 9 |
| 8 |
| 7 |
| 6 |
| 5 |
| 4 |
| 3 |
| 2 |
| 1 |

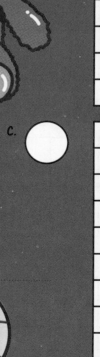

b. ( )
| 10 |
| 9 |
| 8 |
| 7 |
| 6 |
| 5 |
| 4 |
| 3 |
| 2 |
| 1 |

c. ( )
| 10 |
| 9 |
| 8 |
| 7 |
| 6 |
| 5 |
| 4 |
| 3 |
| 2 |
| 1 |

d. ( )
| 10 |
| 9 |
| 8 |
| 7 |
| 6 |
| 5 |
| 4 |
| 3 |
| 2 |
| 1 |

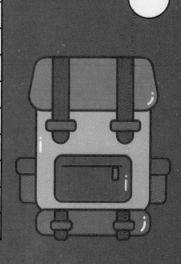

301. Write the weight of given objects.

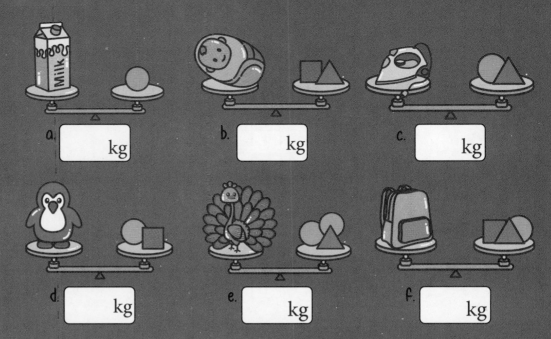

	1kg
△	2kg
■	3kg

a. _____ kg

b. _____ kg

c. _____ kg

d. _____ kg

e. _____ kg

f. _____ kg

302. Solve the word problems and write the answer.

a.
John rode 2 kms on his bike. His sister Sally rode 3000 m on her bike. Who rode the farthest and how much farther did they ride (answer in km)?

1km = 1000m.

b.
A peach weighs 50 g. If you buy 10 peaches and the seller sells it $10 per kg, how much will they cost?

1kg = 1000g.

c.
100 g serving of a breakfast cereal has 1g of salt. How much salt would that be in milligrams?

1g = 1000mg.

d.
Mary buys a spool of thread for sewing. There are 10 m of thread on the spool. She uses 210 cm. How much is left on the spool in centimeters?

1m = 100cm.

303. Tick the shortest one.

a.
1. ☐
2. ☐
3. ☐

b.
1. ☐
2. ☐
3. ☐

c.
1. ☐
2. ☐
3. ☐

304. If the burger is 150 g and the apple is 15 g, how many apples will be equal to the weight of 1 burger?

Measure the Height

305. Measure the height of the given objects and write it in the box.

a. [ ]

b. [ ]

c. [ ]

d. [ ]

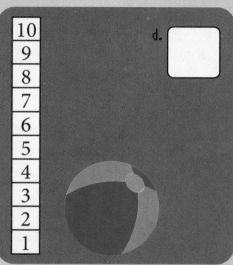

e. [ ]

f. [ ]

306. If 1 feet = 12 inches, convert the following and write the answers.

a. **3** ft ( ) in

d. **6** ft ( ) in

b. **5** ft ( ) in

e. **4** ft ( ) in

c. **2** ft ( ) in

f. **7** ft ( ) in

307. Rank the objects according to their height.

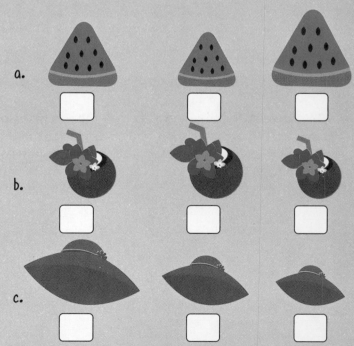

a. [ ] [ ] [ ]

b. [ ] [ ] [ ]

c. [ ] [ ] [ ]

308. Measure the height and write it in the box.

a. ☐ Centimeters

120
110
100
90
80
70
60
50
40
30
20
10

b. ☐ Centimeters

120
110
100
90
80
70
60
50
40
30
20
10

c. ☐ Centimeters

120
110
100
90
80
70
60
50
40
30
20
10

309. If 1cm=10 mm, then calculate the following accordingly.

a. 5cm + 2cm = ☐ mm

b. 3cm + 1cm = ☐ mm

c. 7cm - 5cm = ☐ mm

d. 8cm + 2cm = ☐ mm

e. 4cm - 1cm = ☐ mm

f. 9cm - 4cm = ☐ mm

g. 3cm + 3cm = ☐ mm

310. Measure the height and color the blocks accordingly.

a.

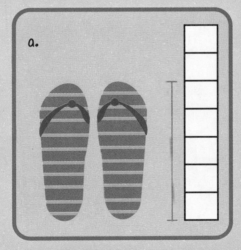

b.

c.

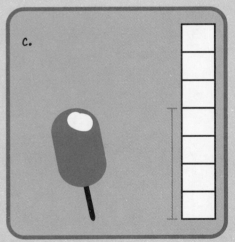

d.

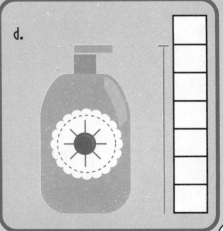

Measure the Weight

311. If 1kg=1000 g, then solve.

a. 5kg + 2kg = [____] g

b. 9kg + 400g = [____] g

c. 2500g + 100g = [____] g

d. 1.5kg + 200g = [____] g

e. 3kg + 400g = [____] g

f. 7kg + 50g = [____] g

312. Observe the scales and then choose which side is heavier?

a.
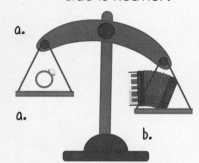
a.   b.

b.
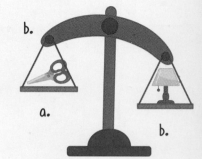
a.   b.

c.
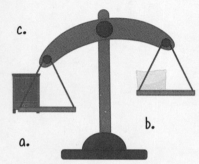
a.   b.

d.
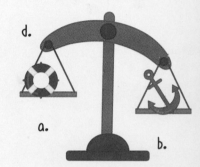
a.   b.

313. Calculate the total weight by using the value given for each fruit.

🍎 20g   🍐 30g   🥝 10g

a.

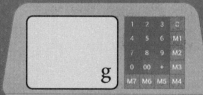
[____] g

b.
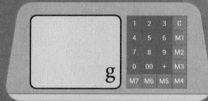

[____] g

c.
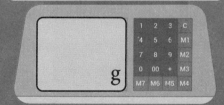

[____] g

d.

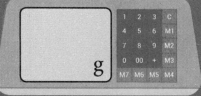
[____] g

e.

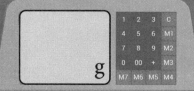
[____] g

f.

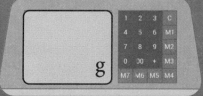
[____] g

314. Fill in the numbers such that the sum of both the sides is equal.

a.
5 2   4 3

5 4 3 2

b.
○ ○   ○ ○

9 5 8 6

c.
○ ○   ○ ○

4 6 5 3

d.
○ ○   ○ ○

9 8 8 7

315. Solve the word problems.

a. Jason purchased 7 kg 200 g of sugar and 9 kg 395 g of rice. What is the total weight which Jason carried?

b. A truck was loaded with 352 kg 100 g of pumpkins and 207 kg 432 g of watermelons. Find the total weight carried by the truck.

c. Father bought 10 kg 750 g of fruits (mangoes and apples). He bought 6 kg 500 g of mangoes. What is the weight of apples?

d. Mary weighs 63 kg 500 g and Alex weighs 59 kg 300 g. Who weighs less and by how much?

316. Choose the correct option to equalise the scale with weights.

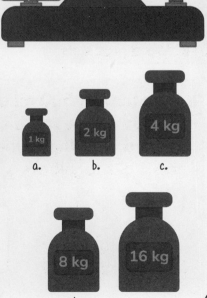

15 kg

1 kg
a.

2 kg
b.

4 kg
c.

8 kg
d.

16 kg
e.

113

Capacity Fun

317. Observe and write the milk level in each bottle.

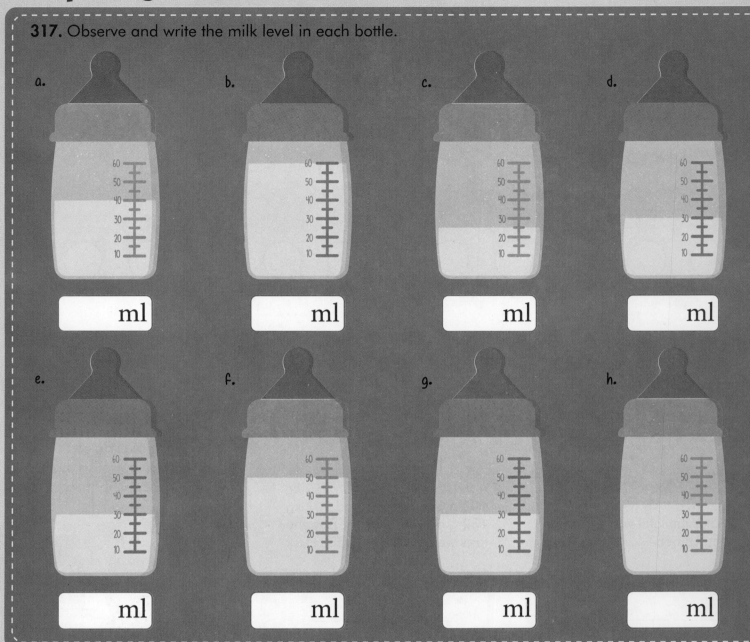

a. _____ ml

b. _____ ml

c. _____ ml

d. _____ ml

e. _____ ml

f. _____ ml

g. _____ ml

h. _____ ml

318. Word problems.

a. Sara bought 500 ml of mustard oil, 250 ml of coconut oil and 2 l of refined oil. What is the total quantity of the 3 oils together?

b. The capacity of the milk boiler is 2 l 500 ml of milk. If 1 l 200 ml of milk is put into the vessel then how much more quantity of milk can be filled in the vessel?

319. Solve and write the answer in ml.

a. $2l + 500ml =$ ⬜

b. $10ml + 50ml =$ ⬜

c. $3l + 100ml =$ ⬜

d. $1l + 1500ml =$ ⬜

e. $4l + 20ml =$ ⬜

320. Write the capacity.

A full teapot can fill 4 tea caps. Find out the capacity of a single cup.

a.
$160ml$ = 🍵🍵🍵🍵   a. 🍵 ⬜

A full teapot can fill 6 tea caps. Find out the capacity of a single cup.

b.
$300ml$ = 🍵🍵🍵🍵🍵🍵   b. 🍵 ⬜

321. Color the number of glasses that can be filled with the juice in the jug.

🥛 $= 100ml$

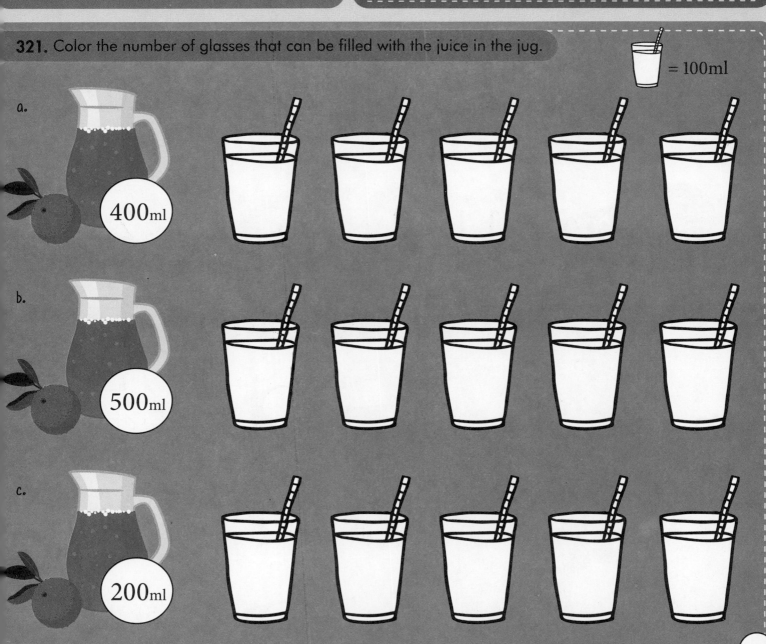

a. $400ml$

b. $500ml$

c. $200ml$

115

Money Games

322. See the price on tags, count the coins and see if you can buy the item. Mark yes or no.

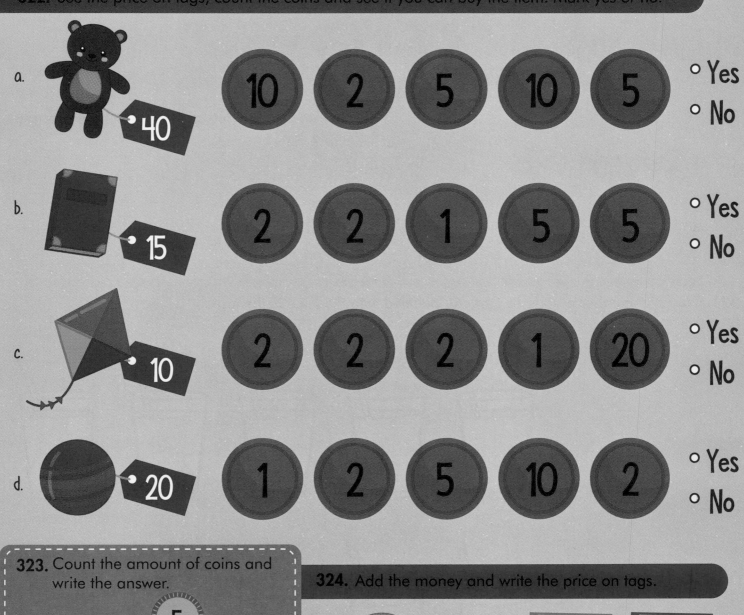

a. 40 | 10 | 2 | 5 | 10 | 5 — ○ Yes ○ No

b. 15 | 2 | 2 | 1 | 5 | 5 — ○ Yes ○ No

c. 10 | 2 | 2 | 2 | 1 | 20 — ○ Yes ○ No

d. 20 | 1 | 2 | 5 | 10 | 2 — ○ Yes ○ No

323. Count the amount of coins and write the answer.

5 5 2 20 20 5 10 1

324. Add the money and write the price on tags.

a. 2 2 2 (TWO) 5 5 5 (FIVE)
    2 2 2 (TWO) 5 5 5 (FIVE)

b. 10 10 10 1 1 1 (ONE)

c. 5 5 5 (FIVE) 1 1 1 (ONE)

325. Each object has a value. Add the values as per the sums and write the total.

$8 $5 $3 $4 $6 $2 $7 $3

a.

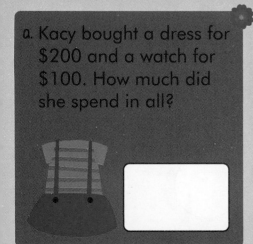

+

What is the total? ----------

b.

+

What is the total? ----------

c.

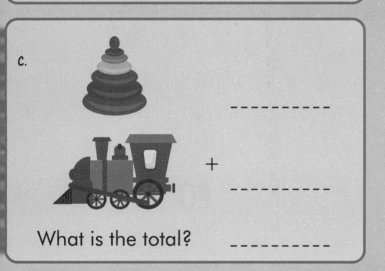

+

What is the total? ----------

d.

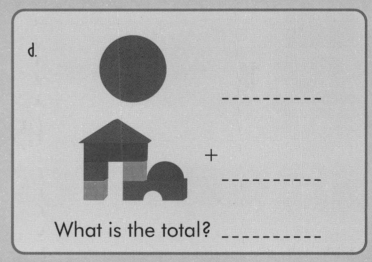

+

What is the total? ----------

326. Word problems.

a. Kacy bought a dress for $200 and a watch for $100. How much did she spend in all?

b. Miles had $600 in her pocket. She spent $50. How much money is left with her?

c. Ken got $50 from his mom, $20 from his father and $10 from his brother. How much money does he have?

Multiplication Fun

327. Fill in the answer and complete the tables.

1	2	3	4	5	6	7	8	9	10
2		6							
3					18				
4									40
5			20						
6						42			
7								63	
8	16								
9				45					
10							80		

328. Write the missing numbers.

a.

$2 \times = 18 \times 2 = $

b.

$ \times 5 = 25 \times = 125$

118

329. Solve the sums and write the answers.

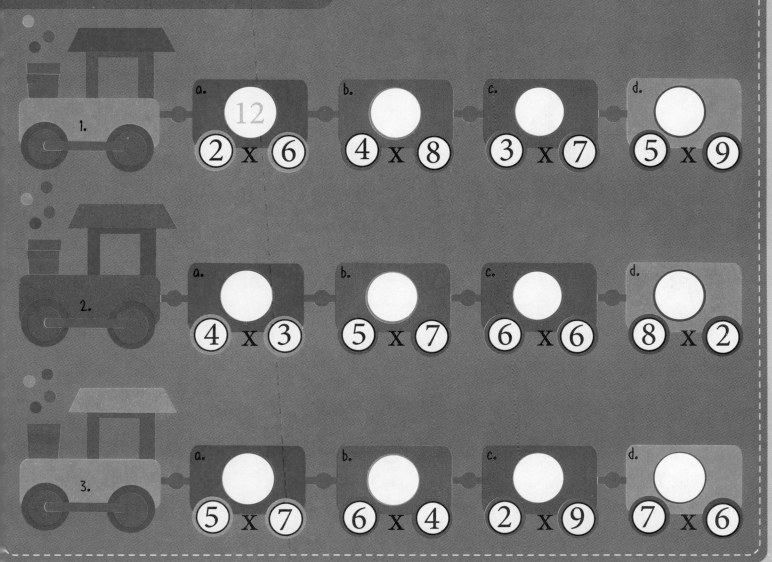

1.
a. 12 2×6
b. 4×8
c. 3×7
d. 5×9

2.
a. 4×3
b. 5×7
c. 6×6
d. 8×2

3.
a. 5×7
b. 6×4
c. 2×9
d. 7×6

330. Look at the images and solve the multiplication sums.

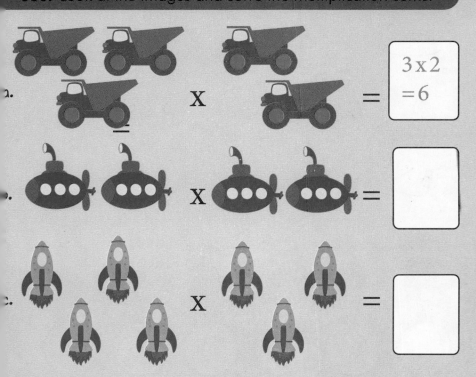

a.   X   = $3 \times 2 = 6$

b.   X   =

c.   X   =

331. Solve the code before the rocket flies.

$2 \times 3 =$

$4 \times 5 =$

$6 \times 7 =$

$8 \times 9 =$

332. Solve the sums on the back of the ladybug.

a. 6 x 5 =

b. 7 x 4 =

c. 8 x 3 =

333. Solve the sums and write answers in the box.

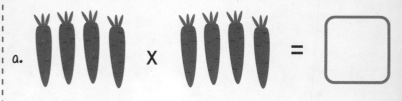

a. [carrots] X [carrots] =

b. [apples] X [apples] =

c. [pears] X [pears] =

d. [strawberries] X [strawberries] =

334. Take hints from the table and solve the sums.

5 x 1 =	1
5 x 2 =	10
5 x 3 =	15
5 x 4 =	20
5 x 5 =	25
5 x 6 =	30
5 x 7 =	35
5 x 8 =	40
5 x 9 =	45

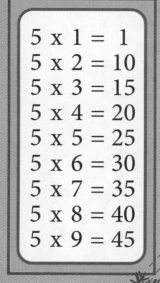

a. b. c. d. e. f. g. h. i.

335. Write the missing numbers.

a. 8 　◯　 24

b. 6 　◯　 18

c. 4 　◯　 12

d. 4 　6　 ◯

e. 5 　◯　 15

336. Solve the word problems.

a. The cost of one scooter is $35,780. What will be the cost of 10 such scooters?

b. A box contains 60 apples. How many apples can be packed in 10 such boxes?

c. The weight of a cement bag is 55 kg. What will be the weight of 100 such bags?

337. Solve the problems and write their answers in the given space.

a.

$9 \times \boxed{} = 18$

$4 \times 2 = \boxed{}$

$\boxed{} \times 5 = 15$

b.

$7 \times 6 = \boxed{}$

$4 \times 9 = \boxed{}$

$3 \times \boxed{} = 12$

c.

$2 \times \boxed{} = 14$

$3 \times 9 = \boxed{}$

$\boxed{} \times 8 = 64$

Division Fun

338. Solve and write.

a. 16 ÷ 2 =

d. 36 ÷ 4 =

b. 27 ÷ 9 =

e. 40 ÷ 5 =

c. 42 ÷ 6 =

f. 56 ÷ 7 =

339. Solve the sums on the snail's back.

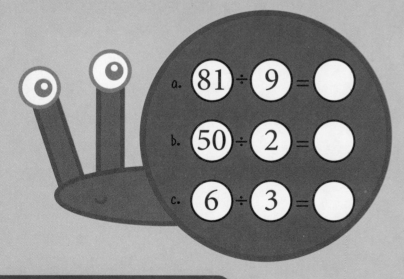

a. 81 ÷ 9 =

b. 50 ÷ 2 =

c. 6 ÷ 3 =

340. Choose the numbers that are divisible by 2.

46	82	74	33	19
55	75	56	16	41
11	15	42	37	53
22	26	95	44	84

341. Solve the sums.

a. 42 ÷ 2 =

b. 88 ÷ 4 =

c. 65 ÷ 5 =

d. 69 ÷ 3 =

e. 72 ÷ 6 =

f. 32 ÷ 8 =

342. Divide the numbers in the center to solve the sums.

a.

$$84 \div 4$$
$$44$$
$$72$$
$$52 \div 4 \div 36 =$$
$$92 \quad 60$$
$$16$$

b.

$$35 \div 5$$
$$65 \quad 10$$
$$80 \div 5 \div 40 =$$
$$95 \quad 70$$
$$25$$

343. Solve and write the answers on the spaceships.

a.

$$81 \div 9$$

b.

$$45 \div 5$$

c.

$$32 \div 4$$

d.

$$60 \div 6$$

e.

$$44 \div 2$$

f.

$$14 \div 7$$

344. Solve the word problems.

a. 96 people have been invited to a banquet. The caterer is arranging tables. Each table can seat 12 people. How many tables are needed?

a. Tom had 63 apples. He divides the apples evenly among 9 friends. How many apples did Tom give to each of his friends?

345. Solve the sums and follow the maze to reach the answers.

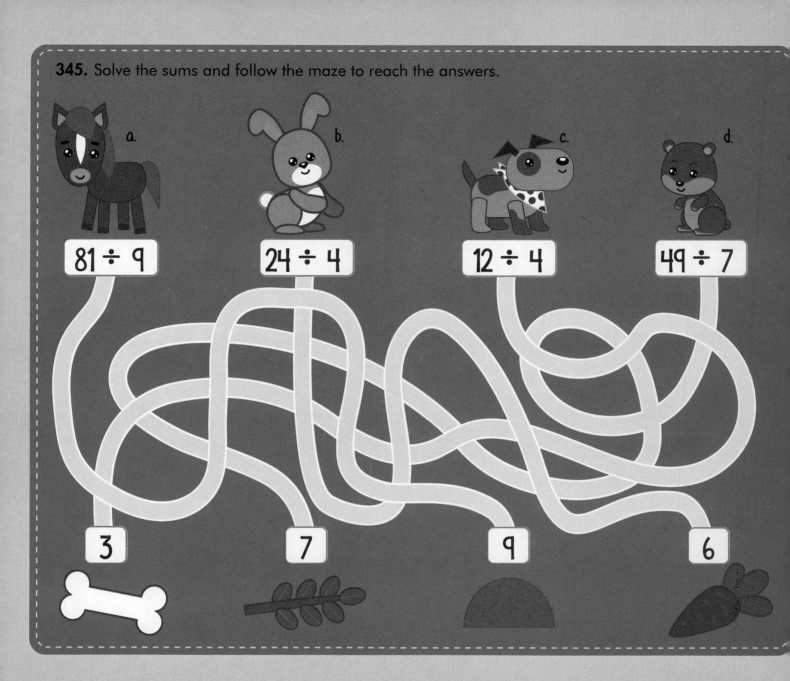

a. $81 \div 9$

b. $24 \div 4$

c. $12 \div 4$

d. $49 \div 7$

3   7   9   6

346. Solve the sums written on the bananas.

a. $21 \div 7$

b. $14 \div 2$

c. $44 \div 4$

347. Practise some more division.

a. $42 \div 2$

b. $66 \div 3$

c. $42 \div 7$

d. $9 \div 9$

e. $20 \div 5$

f. $8 \div 4$

348. Solve the sums and match the questions with the answers.

a. $25 \div 5$

a. 3

b. $24 \div 8$

b. 6

c. $12 \div 2$

c. 5

349. Solve the given problems.

a. There are 15 rows of equal number of dogs. If the total number of dogs are 300, how many dogs are there in each row?

b. 270 carrots were divided between 9 rabbits. How many carrots did each rabbit get?

Data Handling

350. Use the bar graph to answer the questions given below.

Transportation	1	2	3	4	5	6	7	8	9
🚲 bike	■	■	■	■	■	■			
🚗 car	■	■	■	■					
🚌 bus	■	■	■	■	■	■	■		

a. How many kids take bus to school?

b. How many kids ride bike to school?

c. How many kids take car to school?

d. How many kids ride by car and bus in total?

351. Color the graph of the sweets given in the data below.

7				
6				
5				
4				
3				
2				
1				
	🧁	🍫	🧁	🍦

352. Answer the following questions by studying the given data.

a. Count and write.

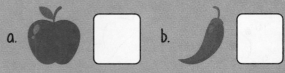

a. 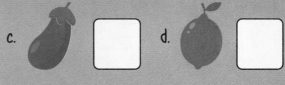 b.

 c. d.

e.

b. Which item do you see the most? Color it.

c. Which item do you see the least? Color it.

d. How many fruits and vegetables are there?

e. How many more apples compared to lemon?

f. Solve the following.

a.  b.

c.  d.

Let's Revise

353. Dot-to-dot.

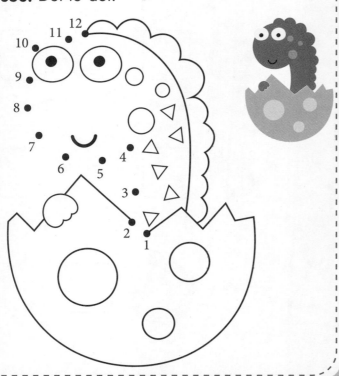

354. Write five more, five less than the number given in the box.

Ten less -5				
41	62	17	55	39
Ten more +5				

Ten less -5				
66	81	29	71	40
Ten more +5				

355. Count and tally.

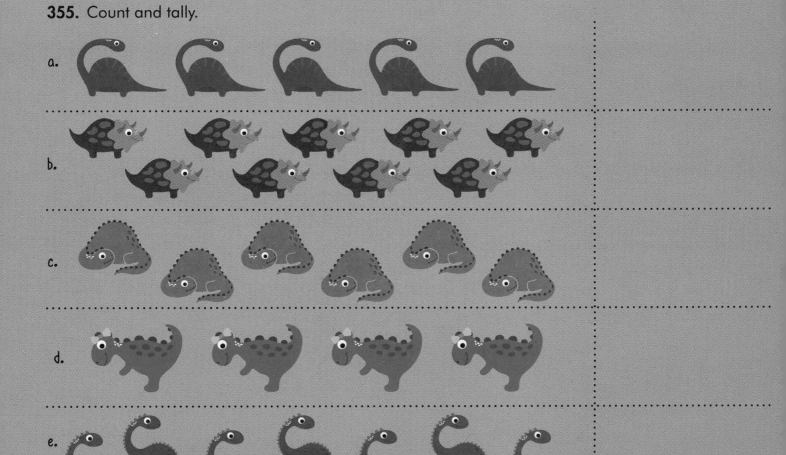

a.

b.

c.

d.

e.

356. Count and write the total of odd and even numbers in the space provided.

Odd ☐ Even ☐

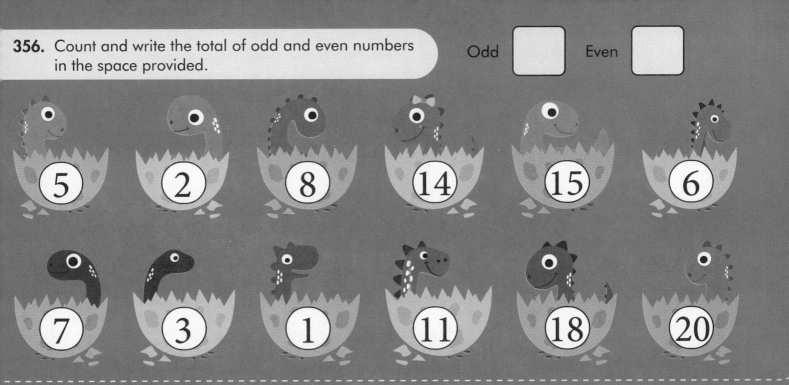

(5) (2) (8) (14) (15) (6)

(7) (3) (1) (11) (18) (20)

357. Solve the sums.

8 +2 10
+7 -9
1

b.
○ +1 ○
+7 -8
2

c.
○ +2 ○
-4 +2
5

d.
○ +1 ○
+3 -4
6

e.
○ -6 ○
+4 +2
4

f.
○ +4 ○
-8 +4
9

g.
○ +9 ○
-2 -7
3

358. Fill in the number wheel. Multiply the number in the center with the numbers in the middle ring.

a. Table of 2

b. Table of 3

c. Table of 4

d. Table of 6

Even numbers in outer ring --

Odd numbers in outer ring --

Color the even numbers red and odd numbers green.

359. Put the given numbers in ascending order (small to big number).

a.
| 327 | 382 |
| 361 | 312 |

b.
| 618 | 655 |
| 624 | 611 |

c.
| 540 | 550 |
| 502 | 569 |

360. Compare the numbers by using >,< or=.

845 ◯ 798

214 ◯ 412

711 ◯ 644

154 ◯ 154

361. Write the expanded form.

a.
234
$200 + 30 + 4$

b.
973
☐ + ☐ + ☐

c.
752
☐ + ☐ + ☐

362. Help mamma bear reach her baby by counting 1-10.

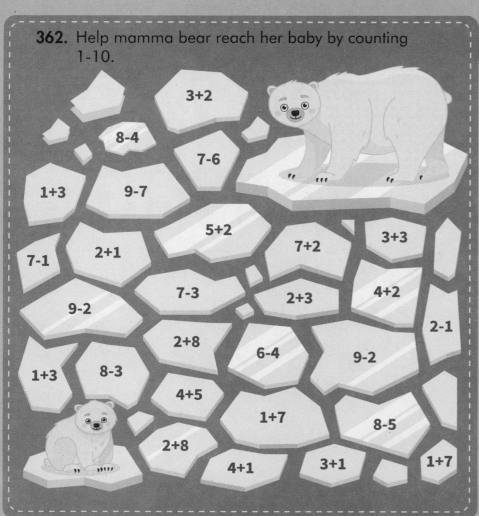

3+2
8-4
7-6
1+3   9-7
5+2
7-1   2+1   7+2   3+3
7-3   2+3   4+2
9-2
2+8   6-4   9-2   2-1
1+3   8-3
4+5
1+7   8-5
2+8
4+1   3+1   1+7

363. Word problems.

a. Sarah and Joey decided to eat cupcakes. Sarah had 2 cupcakes and Joey had 3 cupcakes. How many cupcakes did they eat all together?

b. Akiak left his village with 8 dogs pulling his sled. Along the way, he met his friend Siku and lent him 6 dogs. How many dogs is Akiak left with to pull his sled?

364. Solve and write.

a. 6x5

b. 9-2

c. 4+4

d. 8÷2

e. 7-3

f. 3+4

g. 3x5

h. 9÷3

365. Solve the sums and write in the mug. Also color the mug with even numbers.

a. 10+2 b. 18-11 c. 16+4 d. 11+1

e. 13+5 f. 14+3 g. 19-12

---

366. Color according to the given fractions.

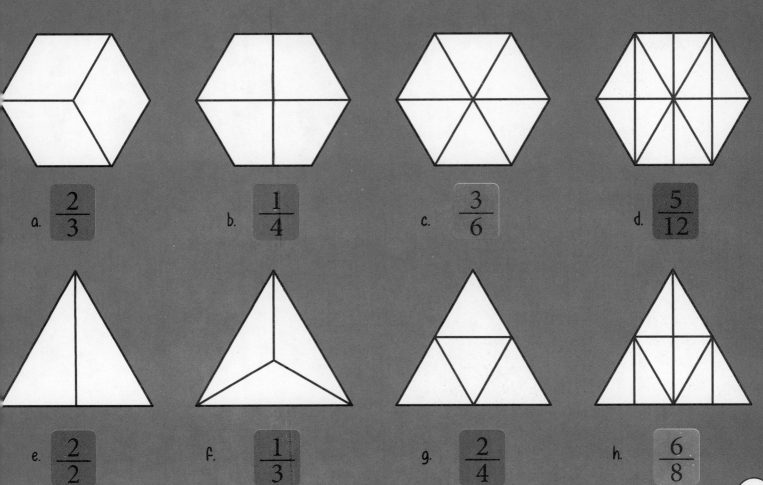

a. $\dfrac{2}{3}$ b. $\dfrac{1}{4}$ c. $\dfrac{3}{6}$ d. $\dfrac{5}{12}$

e. $\dfrac{2}{2}$ f. $\dfrac{1}{3}$ g. $\dfrac{2}{4}$ h. $\dfrac{6}{8}$

Answers

Page No. 6-7

1. Activity
a. 23, 24, 25
b. 55, 56, 57

2. Activity
a. 8, b.12, c.10

3. Activity
a. 4, 6, 8, 10, 12, 14, 16, 18
b. 6, 9, 12, 15, 18, 21, 24

4. Activity
a. 2, b.1

5. Activity
a. 3, b. 6, c. 5
d.5, e. 10, f. 2

6. Activity
a. 4, b. 3, c. 4

Page No. 12-13

19. Activity
a. 10, b. 9
c. 11 d. 15
e.13, f. 16

21. Activity
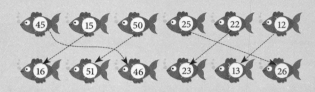
= 1
= 2
= 4
= 3

22. Activity
a. 12
b. 13
c. 9
d. 5

20. Activity

Page No. 8-9

7. Activity
a. 22,23,24,25,26
b. 51,52,53,54,55
c. 72,73,74,75,76
d. 93,94,95,96,97

9. Activity
a. 5,10,15,20
b. 10,20,30,40

10. Activity
7   3   4   5   7

11. Activity
a. 9, b. 3, c. 4, d. 8

Page No. 14-15

23. Activity
a. 6, b. 5 c. 3 d. 2

24. Activity
a. 13, b. 8 c. 16

25. Activity

a. 2, 9
b. 4, 11

26. Activity

Page No. 10-11

14. Activity
a. 6, b. 27

15. Activity
a. 3<42<67<74.
b. 74<67<42<3.

16. Activity
a. 19<27
b. 56>44
c. 34<61
d. 21<30

17. Activity
a. 1. 7<15<23<27<45
   2. 45>27>23>15>7
b. 1. 4<11<20<33<42
   2. 42>33>20>11>4

18. Activity
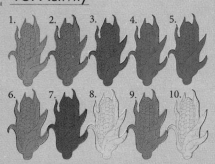

Page No. 16-17

27. Activity
a. 4, 8, 14, 22, 32
b. 4, 7, 12, 19, 28
c. 5, 9, 12, 14, 19
d. 7, 12, 13, 17, 20

28. Activity

29. Activity
a. 3 = 3
b. 5 < 4
c. 6 < 8
d. 1 > 4
e. 9 = 7

31. Activity

31
50

30. Activity
a. 3, b. 4, c. 4, d. 12

32. Activity
a. 7, b. 3, c. 6, d. 11

134

Page No. 18

33. Activity

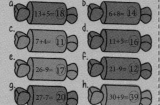

a. 13+5=18 b. 6+8=14
c. 7+4=11 d. 11+5=16
e. 26-9=17 f. 21-9=12
g. 27-7=20 h. 30+9=39

34. Activity

Odd **4** Even **4**

35. Activity

a. **986** Nine hundred and eighty six
_9_ hundreds _8_ tens _6_ ones
_900_ + _80_ + _6_

b. **116** One hundred and sixteen
_1_ hundreds _1_ tens _6_ ones
_100_ + _10_ + _6_

c. **208** Two hundred and eight
_2_ hundreds _0_ tens _8_ ones
_200_ + _0_ + _8_

Page No. 19

36. Activity

a. 13 b. 6 c. 11 d. 7

37. Activity

a. 349 — 40 b. 614 — 600
c. 490 — 0 d. 831 — 30
e. 114 — 10 f. 254 — 200

38. Activity

a. I am 2 8
b. I am 3 6
c. I am 5 1

Page No. 20-21

39. Activity

a. 36, b. 52, c. 24

40. Activity

a. 16, b. 21
c. 10, d. 10

41. Activity

a. 5, b. 7, c. 5
d. 4, e. 7, f. 6

42. Activity

a. 61 62 63 b. 90 91 92
c. 48 49 50 d. 11 12 13
e. 82 83 84 f. 69 70 71

43. Activity

a. 14 (2, 1, 2, 6)
b. 24 (7, 2, 5, 9)
c. 21 (5, 3, 1, 4, 8)
d. 21 (4, 1, 5, 9, 2)

44. Activity

a. 1 (11+7), b. 3 (8-6)
c. 4 (16+9), d. 2 (20-3)

Page No. 22-23

45. Activity

a. 4, b. 11, c. 7
d. 5, e. 9, f. 10

46. Activity

a. 4+2=6, b. 3-2=1, c. 4+1=5

47. Activity

1 + 6 = 7
4 + 2 = 6
5 - 4 = 1

48. Activity

49. Activity

a. 10, b. 3, c. 9
d. 2, e. 7, f. 1

Page No. 24-25

50. Activity

a. 15, b. 13, c. 5, d. 11

51. Activity

a. 7+8 b. 20-2 c. 5+5 d. 14-4
e. 18-3 f. 10+5 g. 12-2 h. 13+2
10 15 18

53. Activity

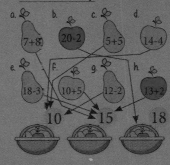

+ = 10
+ = 15
+ = 14
+ = 9

54. Activity

a. b. c.
d. e. f.

55. Activity

a. 24, b. 14, c. 28, d. 12

Page No. 26-27

56. Activity

a. 21, b. 23, c. 37, d. 13

57. Activity

a. 5+4=9, b. 10-5=5
c. 5-4=1, d. 8+3=11

58. Activity

3 +5 8 -2 6 +1 7
7 -2 5 +4 9 -3 6

59. Activity

a. 44, b. 60, c. 48,
d. 60, e. 40, f. 40

61. Activity

a. 4+6 = 8+2
b. 6-1 = 3+2
c. 9-1 = 7+1

62. Activity

a. 20, b. 15, c. 28, d. 8

Page No. 28-29

63. Activity
a. 23, b. 31, c. 37, d. 44, e. 31, f. 22

64. Activity
a. 65, b. 85, c. 98

65. Activity
a. 9, b. 7

66. Activity
a. 6, b. 8, c. 7, d. 8

67. Activity
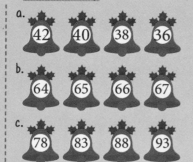

a. 42, 40, 38, 36

b. 64, 65, 66, 67

c. 78, 83, 88, 93

Page No. 30-31

69. Activity
a. 5, b. 7, c. 3, d. 9, e. 6, f. 4

70. Activity
53

71. Activity
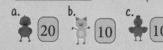
a. 20, b. 10, c. 10

72. Activity
a. 6, b. 6, c. 21, d. 6

73. Activity
a. 13, b. 14, c. 20, d. 45

74. Activity
a. 🍎 =14, b. 🍐 =12,

🍎 + 🍐 = 26

75. Activity
a. 10, 12, 14
b. 15, 17, 19
c. 18, 20, 22

76. Activity
b, d

Page No. 32-33

77. Activity
a. 6524, b. 5017 c. 7340, d. 8431 e. 4683, f. 2565

78. Activity
a. 9

b. 6

c. 3

79. Activity
a. 6, b. 3, c. 4, d.3

80. Activity

Page No. 34-35

82. Activity
a. 5, b. 6, c. 3, d. 5

83. Activity

a. 10-3=7
b. 15-8=7
c. 12-10=10
d. 12-5=7

84. Activity
a. 55, 53, 51, 49, 47
b. 21, 19,17, 15, 13
c. 72, 70, 68, 66, 64
d. 12, 10, 8, 6, 4

85. Activity
a. 3, b. 11, c. 3, d. 13

86. Activity
a. 1, b. 2, c. 1, d. 2

87. Activity
a. 11, b. 7, c. 12

Page No. 36-37

88. Activity
a. 26, 27, 28
b. 50, 51, 52
c. 11, 12, 13

89. Activity
5, 8, 11, 14, 17, 20, 23, 26, 29, 32

93. Activity
a. 9, b. 9

90. Activity

a. >
b. >
c. =
d. <

91. Activity
9 — Nine
6 — Six
12 — Twelve
16 — Sixteen
18 — Eighteen

94. Activity

6, 5, 9

a. Highest = Orange
Lowest = Green

a. Six b. Five, c. Nine

Page No. 38-39

95. Activity
a. 7, b. 5, c. 4, d. 3 e. 3, f. 2, g. 1, h. 3

97. Activity
a. 12, 9, 6
b. 54, 51, 48
c. 37, 34, 31

98. Activity
a. 8, b. 9, c. 6, d. 7

99. Activity

a. 10-5 → 5
b. 14-8 → 6
c. 12-7 → 5
d. 9-3 → 6

136

Page No. 40-41

100. Activity
a. 7, b. 2, c. 4, d. 2 e. 3, f. 3

101. Activity
a. 6, 4, 2
b. 16, 14, 12
c. 12, 10, 8

102. Activity
a. 5-3=2, b. 9-5=4
c. 6-3=3, d. 7-1=6
e. 8-3=5

103. Activity
a. 12, b. 9, c. 12, d. 11

104. Activity
a. 5, b. 6

105. Activity

Page No. 42-43

107. Activity
a. 8th , b. 3rd, c. 5th, d. 2nd

108. Activity
a. 11, b. 8, c. 12, d. 9

109. Activity
a. 8, 6, 4, 2
b. 11, 8, 5, 2
c. 5, 10, 15, 20
d. 3, 7, 11, 15

110. Activity
a. 43, 44, 45, 46, 47
b. 79, 80, 81, 82, 83
c. 22, 23, 24, 25, 26
d. 14, 15, 16, 17, 18

111. Activity

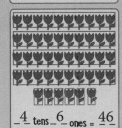

6 tens 4 ones = 64

4 tens 6 ones = 46

Page No. 46-47

119. Activity
a. 2 hundreds 1 tens and 9 ones
b. 7 hundreds 8 tens and 2 ones
c. 4 hundreds 5 tens and 1 ones
d. 6 hundreds 5 tens and 7 ones
e. 3 hundreds 6 tens and 9 ones

118. Activity
a. 15<18, b. 21<27
c. 12>8, d. 16<24

120. Activity
a. 10+2=12 (c)
b. 2+6=8 (d)
c. 12+9=21 (a)
d. 8+8=16 (b)

122. Activity
a. 10, b. 13, c. 7, d. 12

121. Activity

a.

2	8	10	16	25
6	12	14	20	29
10	16	18	24	33

b.

7	16	40	57	78
11	20	44	61	82
15	24	48	65	86

123. Activity

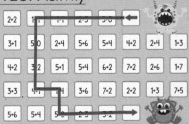

Page No. 48-49

124. Activity

 5 6 4

125. Activity
a. 32<49, b. 99>66
c. 51>15, d. 33<63

126. Activity
a. 15+7=22
b. 37-6=31
c. 42+6=48
d. 29-7=22

128. Activity
a. 12, b. 13

129. Activity
a. 5, b. 3, c. 2

130. Activity
a. 21, b. 19, c. 17, d. 24

127 Activity

  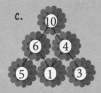

a. 15 / 8 7 / 3 5 2
b. 16 / 9 7 / 6 3 4
c. 10 / 6 4 / 5 1 3

Page No. 50-51

131. Activity
a. 5, b. 5, c. 9, d. 5

132. Activity
a. 9>6
b. 11>9
c. 6<11

135. Activity

133. Activity

a.

11	22	37	40	19
21	32	47	50	29
31	42	57	60	39

b.

1	32	27	79	62
11	42	37	89	72
21	52	47	99	82

Odd 12

Even 4

Page No. 52-53

136. Activity
a. 18, b. 0, c. 6

138. Activity
a. |||| b. ||| |||
c. |||| || d. |||| |||| ||

139. Activity

140. Activity
a. 4, b. 3, c. 2, d. 1
e. 7, f. 8, g. 5, h. 6

141. Activity

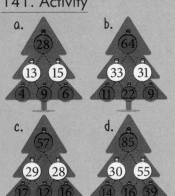

a. 28 / 13 15 / 4 9 6
b. 64 / 33 31 / 11 22 9
c. 57 / 29 28 / 17 12 16
d. 85 / 30 55 / 14 16 39

142. Activity

a.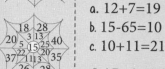

b.

c.

143. Activity

a. 6, 8, 10, 12, 14
b. 6, 9, 12, 15, 18

144. Activity

a. 12+7=19
b. 15-65=10
c. 10+11=21

145. Activity

a. 4, 1.(2x2),
b. 8, 2.(2x4),
c. 12, 4.(2x6),
d. 6, 3.(2x3),

146. Activity

a.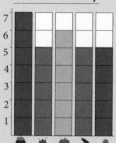
b.

147. Activity

---

160. Activity

1. 7+1=8(d)
2. 9+5=14(f)
3. 4+5=9(c)
4. 6+4=10(e)
5. 8+4=12(b)
6. 3+2=5(a)

161. Activity

a. 18+6=24
b. 4+16=20
c. 11+10=21

162. Activity

a. 8, b. 13, c. 7, d. 14

163. Activity

a. 4, b. 3, c.
5, d. 3, e. 5

164. Activity

a. 14, b. 12,
c. 24

166. Activity

167. Activity

a. 9, 12, 15
b. 7, 10, 13

---

148. Activity

a. 2, 4, 6
b. 1, 3, 5
c. 7, 8, 9

150. Activity

151. Activity

(10) +7 (17) +5 (22) -4 (18) +8 (26) -3 (23)

149. Activity

a. 3<4
b. 8<11
c. 2>1
d. 5<6

153. Activity

a. 3-2=1
b. 4+3=7
c. 4-2=2
d. 2+1=3
e. 3+3=6
f. 3-2=1

---

168. Activity

a. 11<19
b. 21>15
c. 9>6
d. 43>39
e.17<27

169. Activity

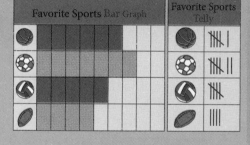

170. Activity

1. 40-15=25(d)
2. 12+10=22(a)
3. 20-3=17(b)
4. 4+5=9(c)

171. Activity

a. 20+10+2=32
b. 30+50+5=85
c. 15+25+40=80
d. 20+40+2=62

172. Activity

---

154. Activity

a. 20, 17, 14, 11
b. 65, 60, 55, 50
c. 42, 36, 30, 24
d. 86, 84, 82, 80

155. Activity

a. 2<3, b. 5>4
c. 4<6, d. 4<5
e.7>5

156. Activity

a. 4-2=2
b. 10+3=13
c. 3+2=5
d. 3-2=1

158. Activity

a. 20+3=23, 150-23=127
b. 10+20+25=55
c. Jacket and Socks
d. 25+12=37

159. Activity

a. 7-2=5
b. 6-4=2
c. 8-5=3

---

173. Activity

a. 32, b. 56
c. 22, d. 12

174. Activity

a. 64, b. 48
c. 51, d. 38, e. 32

175. Activity

a. 4 tens 3 ones=43
b. 5 tens 5 ones=55
c. 2 tens 3 ones=23
d. 2 tens 2 ones=22

176. Activity

a. 36 / 9 / 27 — 3 tens 6 ones

b. 63 / 52 / 11 — 6 tens 3 ones

c. 59 / 35 / 24 — 5 tens 9 ones

177. Activity

a. 32, b. 17, c. 30, d. 40

179. Activity
a. 6, b. 4

180. Activity
a. 4+3=7, b. 5-2=3
c. 3+3=6, d. 9-5=4

181. Activity
a. 21, b. 21, c. 25

183. Activity
a. 4x8=32, b. 6x6=36,
c. 2x6=12

184. Activity
a. 6, b. 9 c. 5

182. Activity
a. 5+6+1
5 hundreds 6 tens 1 ones
b. 4+9+8
4 hundreds 99 tens 8 ones
c. 3+2+1
3 hundreds 2 tens 1 ones

178. Activity

185. Activity
a. 2 + 2 → 4
b. 4 + 2 → 6
c. 3 + 2 → 5
d. 5 + 3 → 8

186. Activity
a. 12 4
b. 6 16
16 7 5 22 9 5
c. 12
d. 14

187. Activity
b. 8+6=14

188. Activity
a. 5+4=9, b. 3+7=10,
c. 6+1=7

189. Activity

5 4 5
a. 10+10=20,
b. 4+10=14,
c. 10+8=18

190. Activity
a. 15, 16, 17, 18
b. 22, 27, 32, 37
c. 65, 75, 85, 95

192. Activity
a. 6, b. 7, c. 3
d. 2, e. 4, f. 5

193. Activity
a. 4, 8, 12, 16
b. 20, 40, 60, 80

194. Activity
a.

33 29
b.
54 45

195. Activity
a. Color the 4th circle pink and the 6th circle blue.

b. Color the 5th triangle red and the 1st triangle
c. Color the 3rd star and the 2nd star

196. Activity
a. 0, b. 4, c. 3, d. 4
e. 5, f. 5, g. 6, h. 4

197. Activity
a. ☐ 10, b. ◯ 6
c. △ 6, d. ◯ 2

199. Activity
a. ☆, b. ◯
c. ☐, d. ◯
e. ▭

198. Activity
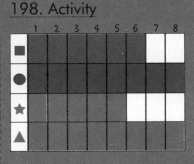

200. Activity
a. ☐ 7, b. ◯ 4
c. △ 7

201. Activity
a. ☐ (4), b. (3)
c. ☐ (4), d. ☆ (5)
e. ⬠ (5)

202. Activity
1. 3+8=11
2. 9-2 =7
3. 6+3=9
♥ =9, ⬠ =3, ◇ =3

203. Activity
a. ☐, b. ⬠
c. △, d. ⬠

204. Activity
a. ☐ 1 △ 3 ⬡ 1
b. ☐ 3 ◯ 5 △ 1

205. Activity
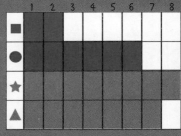
a. Star, b. ☐ Square

206. Activity
a. ☐ 8, b. ◯ 4
c. △ 10

208. Activity
a. Triangle
b. Circle
c. Square
d. Rectangle
e. Star

209. Activity

210. Activity
a. ☐ 12, b. ◇ 6
c. ☆ 10, d. △ 17
e. ▭ 3, f. ◯ 6

211. Activity

a. 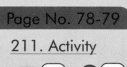 5 b. ● 5

c. ▲ 4 d. ⬭ 1

212. Activity

a. ▢ 3

b. ▢ 4

c. ⬭ 2

213. Activity

a. Square ▢
b. Pentagon ⬠
c. Triangle ▲
d. Hexagon ⬡
e. Octagon ⯃
f. Rectangle ▭

214. Activity

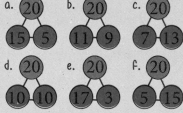

215. Activity

216. Activity

217. Activity

a. 12-5=7(b)
b. 6+6=12(a)
c. 10+5=15(c)

218. Activity

a. 11+7=18
b. 9+6=15
c. 15+8=23

219. Activity

a. 4, 8, 12, 16, 20, 24
b. 7, 14, 21, 28, 35, 42

220. Activity

a. 10+10+2=22
b. 7+8-2=13
c. 10-5+8=13
d. 14-5+8=17

222. Activity

a. Dogs 12
b. Cats 14

223. Activity

a. 67 / 76 77 78 / 87
b. 11 / 20 21 22 / 31
c. 56 / 65 66 67 / 76
d. 25 / 34 35 36 / 45

224. Activity

a. 11+8=19
b. 22-5=17
c. 11+4=15
d. 15-3=12
e. 28-7=21

225. Activity

a. 6, b. 5, c. 5, d. 4

226. Activity

a. 20 / 15 5
b. 20 / 11 9
c. 20 / 7 13
d. 20 / 10 10
e. 20 / 17 3
f. 20 / 5 15

227. Activity

a. 8 = ||||| |||
b. 11= ||||| ||||| |
c. 14 = ||||| ||||| ||||
d. 7= ||||| ||

228. Activity

a. 3:00, b. 10:45
c. 9:30, d. 8:15

228. Activity

230. Activity

a. 06:00 b. 07:00
c. 12:00 d. 03:00

231. Activity

a. 12:45 b. 03:00

232. Activity

a. 7:15 b. 2 hours , c. 4:00 pm
d. 7:30, e. 7 hours 30 minutes
f. 7 hours

233. Activity

a. half past 7, b. half past 3
c. half past 12, d. half past 10

234. Activity

a. 8 O' Clock, b. 5 O' Clock
c. 7 O' Clock, d. 2 O' Clock

235. Activity

a. 2:45 Quarter to three
b. 10:30 Half past ten
c. 7:00 Seven O' clock
d. 6:15 Quarter past six

236. Activity

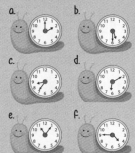

237. Activity

a. 9:30 - 10:30 - 11:30
b. 4:15 - 5:15 - 6:15
c. 10:00 - 11:00 - 12:00
d. 3:45 - 4;45 - 5:45

238. Activity

a. quarter past 1, 1:15
b. quarter past 10, 10:15
c. quarter past 5, 5:15
d. quarter past 7, 7:15

239. Activity

240. Activity

a. quarter to8, 7:45
b. quarter to 3, 2:45
c. quarter to 6, 5:45
d. quarter to 12, 11:45

242. Activity

a. 30 minutes
b. 35 minutes
c. 20 minutes
d. 5 minutes

243. Activity

a. 7:00
b. 5:00

Page No. 90-91

244. Activity

a. b. c. d.

245. Activity
a. 8 O' Clock
b. 10 O' Clock
c. 2 O' Clock
d. 9 O' Clock
e. 5 O' Clock
f. 1 O' Clock

246. Activity
a. 3:35, b. 4:40, c. 12:20pm
d. 2hours and 2 minutes,
e. 4:10, f. 7:16

247. Activity
a. 1:30 - 2:00 - 2:30
b. 7:30 - 8:00 - 8:30
c. 3:30 - 4:00 - 4:30
d. 10:30 - 11:00 - 11:30

248. Activity
a. 60, b. 60, c. 24, d. 7, e. 52
f. 12, g. 365 &1/4, h. 4

250. Activity
a. 1:15, b. 8:00, c. 2:15
d. 5:00, e. 11:05, f. 9:30

Page No. 91

249. Activity
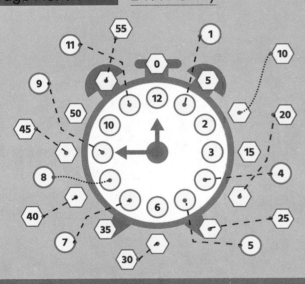

Page No. 92-93

251. Activity
a.  b.
40 15
35 8 3 25
5
45 6 50
15 30

12 32
20 8 6 24
4
8 9 16
36 40

252. Activity
a. 4 Tens, b. 6 Hundred
c. 2 Hundred, d. 5 ones
e. 2 ones, f. 9 tens

253. Activity
a. 6x6=36, b. 12x2=24
c. 6x12=72, d. 6x4=24
e. 24x12=288, f. 4x6=24

254. Activity
(9) + (5) = (14)
(7) - (5) = (2)
(2) (10) = (12)

255. Activity
a. 12, b. 9, c. 8, d. 5 hours

256. Activity
a. 5x3= 15, b. 3x4=12,
c. 4x1=4, d. 5x4=20,
e. 1x5=5, f. 2x5=10

Page No. 94-95

257. Activity
a.  = 2
b. = 2
c. ? = 1

258. Activity

259. Activity

3 5
5 4
a. 3+4+5=12
b. 5+3+5=13
c. 5+4+4=13
d. 3+5+5=13
e. 5+5+3=13

260. Activity
a. 15, 25, 35, 45, 55
b. 7, 14, 21, 28, 35
c. 9, 18, 27, 36, 45
d. 12, 16, 20, 24, 28

261. Activity
a. Lily, b. yellow,
c. fifth, d. Lotus

262. Activity
a. 7, b. 11
c. 5, d. 3

263. Activity
a. 469, b. 10
c. 600

Page No. 96-97

264. Activity

5 6
4 5
b. Red fish
e. Green fish

265. Activity
a. ||, b. |
c. ||, d. |||
e. Yellow fish/
star fish

266. Activity
 50% 10%
25% 15%
c. 30 , d. 70

267. Activity
 20 30 15
10 25
a. 10+25+30=65
b. 20+15+25=60
c. 30+30+10=75
d. 25+20+10=55
e. 15+10+30=55

Page No. 98-99

268. Activity
a. 1/4, b. 2/4
c. 5/8, d. 3/4

269. Activity
a. 3/5, b. 2/8
c. 1/3, d. 1/4
e. 3/5

271. Activity
a. 5/8, b. 2/4
c. 4/12, d. 2/5
e. 1/3 f. 2/6

272. Activity

a. b. c. d. e.

273. Activity

a. < b. <
c. > d. <

Page No. 100-101

274. Activity
a. 1/3, b. 1/4
c. 2/3, d. 2/9
e. 4/5, f. 1/4

275. Activity
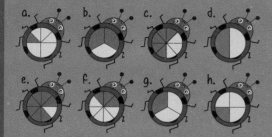
a. b. c. d.
e. f. g. h.

276. Activity
a. 4/6, b. 3/5
c. 2/5, d. 3/4
e. 1/4, f. 2/4

277. Activity
a. 3/10, b. 2/7
c. 5/12

278. Activity
a. 3/6, b. 3/6
c. 4/6, d. 5/6
e. 4/6, f. 1/6

Page No. 106-107

292. Activity
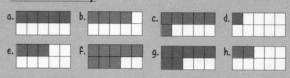
a. 5/7
b. 2/5
c. 4/6
d. 1/5
e. 3/7

293. Activity
a. 6/8, b. 2/8
c. 4/8, d. 3/8

294. Activity
a. 8/9, b. 4/5, c. 6/7

295. Activity
a. 4, b. 6

296. Activity

a. b. c. d.
e. f. g. h.

Page No. 102-103

279. Activity
a. 1/2, b. 4/12
c. 5/8, d. 1/3
e. 4/6, f. 4/7

280. Activity
a. 16/10=8/5(f), b. 9/6=3/2 (b)
c. 4/6=2/3(a), d. 2/6=1/3(e)
e. 8/14=4/7(c), f. 14/35=2/5(d)
g. 5/10=1/2(g), h. 20/12=5/3(i)
j.10/2=5/1(k), k. 5/5=1(h)

284. Activity
a. 1/2>1/3, b. 4/12<5/12, c. 3/4>1/4, d. 2/3>1/3
e. 1/2<3/4, f. 2/4>2/5

281. Activity
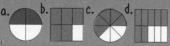
a. b. c.
3/4   5/8   2/3

282. Activity
a. 4/9, b. 12/22

283. Activity
a. 3/6, b. 5/8, c. 2/6,
d. 2/4, e. 1/2, f. 3/4

Page No. 108-109

297. Activity
a. 7000m, b. 9400m
c. 2600m, d. 1700m
e. 3400m

298. Activity

a. 7, b. 5, c. 1, d. 4, e. 8,
f. 8, g. 3, h. 6,

299. Activity
a. B, b.B, c. A, d. A

300. Activity
a. 8, b. 5, c. 4, d. 7

301. Activity
a. 1 kg, b. 5 kg
c. 3 kg, d. 4kg
e. 4 kg, f. 6 kg

302. Activity
a. 1 km, b. 5o rupees,
c. 1000mg, d. 790cm

303. Activity
a. 2, b.1, c. 3

304. Activity
a. 10

Page No. 104-105

285. Activity
1. a. 5/6, b. 3/7 c. 4/6, d. 2/7
2. a. 1/4, b. 3/4 c. 2/4, d. 0/4
3. a. 8/10, b. 4/10 c. 6/10,
d. 5/10

286. Activity

a. b. c. d. e.

287. Activity
1. 1/4 = 4/16, 2/8
2. 1/3= 6/18, 5/15, 4/12,
2/6, 3/9
3. 1/2= 6/12, 3/6, 5/10, 7/14,
8/16, 2/4, 4/8

288. Activity
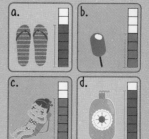
a. b. c. d.

289. Activity
a. 3/6, b. 3/7, c.1/4

290. Activity
a. 3/6<5/6, b. 3/5<4/5
c. 1/8>3.5/8, d. 4/5<4.5/5
e. 2/6=1/3, f. 6/8>2/4

291. Activity
a. 3/16, b. 3/8, c.2/4
d. 4/9, e. 1/4, f.2/6
g. 1/8, h. 2/8

Page No. 110-111

305. Activity
a. 7, b. 6, c. 8, d. 4, e. 7, f. 8

306. Activity
a. 36 in, b. 60 in , c. 24 in
d. 72 in, e. 48 in, f. 84 in

307. Activity
a. 2,1,3
b. 2,3,1
c. 3,2,1

308. Activity
a. 85 cm, b.100 cm
c. 75 cm

309. Activity
a. 70 mm, b. 40 mm
c. 20 mm, d.100 mm
e. 30 mm, f.50 mm
g.60 mm

310. Activity
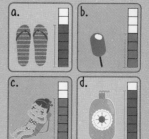
a. b.
c. d.

Page No. 112-113

311. Activity
a. 7000g, b. 9400g
c. 2600g, d. 1700g
e. 3400g, f. 7050g

312. Activity
a. b, b. b, c. a, d. b

313. Activity
a. 60g, b. 50g
c. 60g, d. 70g
e. 70g, f. 100g

314. Activity
a. 5+2=4+3
b. 9+5=8+6
c. 5+4=6+3
d. 9+7=8+8

315. Activity
a. 16kg 595g
b. 559kg 532g
c. 4kg 250g apples
d. Alex weighs less and 4kg 200g

316. Activity
8kg + 4kg + 2kg + 1kg

Page No. 118-119

327. Activity

1	2	3	4	5	6	7	8	9	10
2	4	6	8	10	12	14	16	18	20
3	6	9	12	15	18	21	24	27	30
4	8	12	16	20	24	28	32	36	40
5	10	15	20	25	30	35	40	45	50
6	12	18	24	30	36	42	48	54	60
7	14	21	28	35	42	49	56	63	70
8	16	24	32	40	48	56	64	72	80
9	18	27	36	45	54	63	72	81	90
10	20	30	40	50	60	70	80	90	100

328. Activity
a. 2x9=18x2=36
b. 5x5=25x5=125

329. Activity
1. a.12, b. 32, c. 21, d. 45
2. a.12, b. 35, c. 36, d. 16
3. a.35, b. 24, c. 18, d. 42

330. Activity
a. 3x2=6, b. 2x2=4
c. 4x3=12

331. Activity
a. 2x3=6
b. 4x5=20
c. 6x7=42
d 8x9=72

Page No. 114-115

317. Activity
a. 40ml, b. 60ml
c. 25ml,, d. 30ml
e. 30ml, f. 50ml
h. 35ml

318. Activity
a. 2L and 750 ml
b.1L and 300ml

319. Activity
a. 2500 ml, b. 60 ml
c. 3100 ml, d. 2500 ml
e. 4020 ml

320. Activity
a. | 40 ml |
b. | 50 ml |

321. Activity

a.
b.
c.

Page No. 120-121

332. Activity
a. 6x5=30
b. 7x4=28
c. 8x3=24

333. Activity
a. 4x4=16, b. 5x2=10
c. 3x6=18, d 5x3=15

334. Activity
a. 5x1=5, b. 5x2=10
c. 5x3=15, d. 5x4=20
e. 5x5=25, f. 5x6=30
g. 5x7=35, h. 5x8=40
i. 5x9=45

335. Activity
a. 8,16, 24, b. 6,12,18
c. 4, 8, 12, d. 4,6, 8
d. 5, 10, 15

336. Activity
a. Rs 3,57,800
b. 600 apples
c. 5500 kg

337. Activity
a. 9×2=18, 4×2=8,
 3×5=15
b. 7×6=42, 4×9=36,
 3×4=12
c. 2×7=14, 3×9=27,
 8×8=64

Page No. 116-117

322. Activity
a. No, b. Yes
c. Yes, d. Yes

323. Activity
68

324. Activity
a. 14, b. 11, c. 6

325. Activity
a. 8+3=11
b. 4+7=11
c. 2+6=8
d. 3+5=8

326. Activity
a. Rs.300
b. Rs.550
c. Rs.80

Page No. 122-123

338. Activity
a. 16÷2=8, b. 27÷9=3
c. 42÷6=7, d. 36÷4=9
e. 40÷5=8, f. 56÷7=8

339. Activity
a. 81÷9=9
b. 50÷2=25
c. 6÷3=2

340. Activity

46	82	74	33	19
55	75	56	16	41
11	15	42	37	53
22	26	95	44	84

341. Activity
a. 42÷2=21, b. 88÷4=22
c. 65÷5=13, d. 69÷3=23
e. 72÷6=12, f. 32÷8=9

343. Activity
a. 81÷9=9, b. 45÷5=9
c. 32÷4=8, d. 60÷6=10
e. 44÷2=22, f. 14÷7=2

344. Activity
a. 96÷12=8 Tables
b. 63÷9=7 apples to
each friend

342. Activity

a.
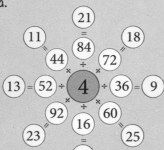

b.

---

345. Activity

a. 81÷9=9, b. 24÷4=6
c. 12÷4=3, d. 49÷7=7

346. Activity

a. 21÷7=3, b. 14÷2=7
c. 44÷4=11

347. Activity

a. 42÷2=21, b. 66÷3=22
c. 42÷7=6, d. 9÷9=1
e. 20÷5=4, f. 8÷4=2

348. Activity

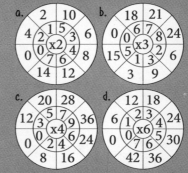

349. Activity

a. 300÷15=20
20 dogs in each row.
b. 270÷9=3
3 carrots for 1 rabbit

---

350. Activity

a. 7 kids, b. 5 kids
c. 3 kids, d. 10 kids

351. Activity

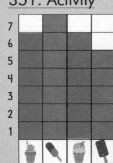

352. Activity

a.

b.

c.

d. 7+5+5+6+4=27
e. 7-6=1
f. a. 7+7=5=19
   b. 6+7+5=18
   c. 7+5+6=18
   d. 4+4+4=12

---

354. Activity

a.

36	57	12	50	34
41	62	17	55	39
46	67	22	60	44

b.

61	76	24	66	35
66	81	29	71	40
71	86	34	76	45

355. Activity

a. |||| |||
b. |||| |||| |||
c. |||| ||||
d. |||||
e. |||| | ||

356. Activity

Odd 7   Even 6

357. Activity

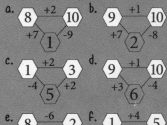

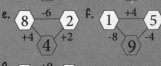

---

358. Activity

a.
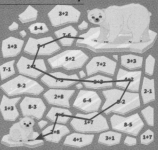

Even number 24
Odd number 4

359. Activity

a. 312<327<361<382
b. 611<618<624<655
c. 502<540<550<569

360. Activity

a. 845>798
b. 214<412
c. 711>644
d. 154=154

361. Activity

a. 200 + 30 + 4
b. 900 + 70 + 3
c. 700 + 50 + 2

---

363. Activity

a. 2+3=5, 5 Cupcakes
b. 8-6=2, 2 dogs

364. Activity

a. 6x5=30, b. 9-2=7
c. 4+4=8, d. 8÷2=4
e. 7-3=4, f. 3+4=7
g. 3x5=15, h. 9÷3=3

365. Activity

a. 10+2=12, b.18-11=7
c. 16+4=20, d. 11+1=12
e. 13+5=18, f. 14+3=17
g. 19-12+7

362. Activity

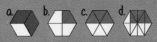

366. Activity

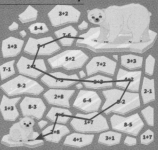
